Into Darkness

Audrey Brice

AN ORDO TEMPLI SERPENTIS MYSTERY

Darkerwood Publishing Group
United States of America

Darkerwood Publishing Group
Colorado, U.S.A.
First Paperback Printing, March 2012 - U.S.A.

ISBN: 978-0978897536
0978897536

For Wheezy and Tammy. All writers need supporters and this book needed a great deal of support, so thank you both for the encouragement.

CHAPTER ONE
SATURDAY, JUNE 24

The beginning was the end. Of all the stupid things I could have thought at the end of my life, this was it. I felt the clay Lucifuge amulet I wore press hard against my left breast, reminding me that it was because of those damn amulets I was in this mess to begin with. Beneath me the unyielding rocky ground dug into my flesh. Above me, the psychopath who'd murdered Mike loaded the gun.

But I digress. How I ended up the victim of another murderer in the short span of a few months is a longer story.

My name is Elizabeth Tanner and I'm a magician. The story I'm about to tell you is true.

Only a few short weeks ago I sat at my dining room table carving sigils into clay amulets. It's a little tradition of mine; something I do around every summer solstice. Michael, Mike, my sexy detective boyfriend who I'd hooked up with after my last entanglement with a killer, was working that Saturday on a theft case, so I was home alone. Like usual I had CNN on in the background.

The clay I was using had a faux metallic sheen to it, giving the clay disks I was working on the illusion of metal. As I carved I mused at how, for centuries, humans had believed in the power of magickal talismans to do everything from repel evil to bring good health. I've always thought there's something comforting in a talisman. For me, there's something even more comforting in the act of constructing them. I enjoy feeling them between my palms as I imbue them with the essence of their design. Every year I make about fifty or so to give to friends. This often satiates my talisman making lust until the next summer solstice comes around. The most interesting thing about talismans, however, is sometimes they're not always what they seem to be.

When I'd finished carving the last one I got up and went into the kitchen to pre-heat the oven. I've often thought whoever invented oven-bake clay was a genius. It made a magician's work that much easier when it came to creating certain tools.

It was directly after I'd turned on the oven that my cell phone rang. I didn't bother looking at the caller ID even though the ring tone suggested it wasn't anyone I knew. Probably a wrong number. I was feeling cavalier so I answered anyway. "Hello!"

"Ms. Elizabeth Tanner?" an older woman's voice asked.

For a second she almost sounded like my mother. "Speaking."

"My name is Marjorie Ellis and I need your help," the woman started.

"May I ask how you got my name and number?" I didn't want to be rude, but it wasn't the habit of strangers to call my cell phone and ask me for help.

"Oh, of course, I'm sorry," the woman apologized as if giving me that background information hadn't occurred to her. "Mel Davis gave me your number. I'm a solitary Daemonolatress in Fort Collins and I need someone to dispose of some unique Daemonolatry items for me. Things I no longer want. Mel said you could help me with that."

"Oh!" I said, finally realizing who Mel was. Mel was one of many solitary Daemonolaters along the front-range who weren't regularly involved with any of the established groups. We called them solitaries or solitary practitioners. There were many solitaries who were still members of The Order. "Okay, I didn't mean to sound so confused. I just haven't talked to Mel since last Yule," I explained clumsily, then got to the point. "What kind of items?"

"Well," the woman started. I could sense some uncertainty in her voice. "I was with a man for a few years and we practiced together. He gave me a few things very Daemonolatry specific. A mantel clock engraved with the sigil of Lucifer, a few talismans, a lap board he made me and a really beautiful old altar. We split up recently and I really don't want them anymore. Too many painful memories attached if you know what I mean. Would you come get them?"

I thought about telling her to just put up an advertisement on one of the online message boards because I knew she could easily get rid of the stuff herself, but I had to admit I was interested in the altar, the lap board, and the clock. The altar because mine was getting a bit rickety, the spirit board because I collected them, and the clock because I didn't have a mantel clock and quite frankly, my mantel was bare except for some family and friend photos in mismatched frames. Not to mention that if they turned out to be items I didn't want, I certainly had the connections to get rid of the stuff quickly. "Well," I started.

"I know I could just advertise them online myself, but I really just want this stuff out of my house because I'm moving and you're more centrally located. I don't even want money for them," she said quickly.

A little too quickly. "What's the catch?" I asked carefully.

She let out a nervous laugh. "You'd have to drive up to Fort Collins and pick it up. If you do that, all of it's yours to get rid of however you see fit!"

"Fair enough." I smiled, kind of excited at the prospect of a new altar. I took down her address and phone number and told her Mike and I would drive out the following day.

"You won't change your mind will you?" she asked before we hung up.

"I'll be there," I assured her. We said our goodbyes and I hung up, all the while shrugging off the familiar tugging sensation twisting in my gut.

I wandered into the bathroom of my small, three bedroom, ranch-style house that I'd bought with money my grandfather left me. Flipping on the light, I looked at myself in the mirror. I felt the tug again.

There was a brief flash of light. I had the sensation I was being sucked out of my body only to find myself standing in darkness, surrounded by swirling gray smoke. I heard strange noises in the dark around me and to my right a hiss emerged from the murk.

Turning toward it I stopped short when I spotted two red eyes looking at me. "You really are a masochist, aren't you?" She said.

I couldn't really see the Daemon, just the faint outline of a humanoid-like creature. "I, I don't know what you m-mean," I stammered like an idiot.

"You know exactly what I mean, Elizabeth. You never listen to me," the Daemon chastised. "You deal with this now or you will suffer for it."

And just like that, with a dizzying jolt, I found myself falling backward onto my bathroom floor. I hit with a thud, catching myself with my hands and my right hip. When I realized I was okay and not in as much pain as I expected, I looked up. The first thing I saw was the painting of Levi's Baphomet one of my friends had done for me. It hung over the towel rack. Done in black, gray, and red, it matched the rest of the dark art hanging throughout my house. See, I'm somewhat a collector of dark art being that I'm a Daemonolatress, so finding myself in a trance and speaking to Daemons isn't abnormal for me. Not by a longshot. The Daemonic speaks to me on a regular basis, in fact.

I hoisted myself to my feet, splashed some cold water on my face and wandered back into the kitchen, noting the house probably needed a good sprucing up. Maybe that's what the Daemon meant when she said I needed to deal with it? After all, I'm certainly not the domestic type. I'm not super messy, but my house is never really tidy either. Letting out a deep sigh, I shook my head.

Of course that wasn't what the Daemon meant and I knew it. What was I supposed to deal with? I hated how cryptic the Daemons often were. Usually they'd give me messages and if it wasn't apparent what they were trying to say, it became apparent in hindsight. Needless to say, being a medium isn't all it's cracked up to be. If the Daemons weren't stepping in with something to say, the dead were. I could usually tune the dead out, and often did, but if the Daemons wanted your attention – they got it.

The TV was still blaring CNN. It was the only thing I ever watched. After getting myself another cup of coffee and putting the talismans in the oven, I settled on the couch and waited for the oven timer to go off. Eventually the Daemons would reveal to me what I needed to know, so I decided not to worry about it.

CHAPTER TWO
SUNDAY, JUNE 25

The next morning I grabbed two water bottles, filled them from the filtered water dispenser, and set them on the counter. Mike had the GPS at the dining room table and his long, thick fingers were attempting to program in the Fort Collins address. "Damn it! I need to get you a new GPS."

"One you can work?" I asked with a giggle.

He gave me a wry look and continued playing with it. "I keep hitting the wrong buttons. This was made for people with small fingers. Okay, here we go."

I started going through my checklist. "Purse, keys, water, GPS, you, and me. Did I miss anything?"

Mike's dark eyes playfully looked into mine and he shook his head. "We have everything. Let's go."

We ultimately decided to take my Subaru because it was bigger and could hold the altar. I handed the keys to Mike. It just didn't seem right that he was the man and I'd be driving, so I was happy to relinquish the duty to him. I know, I know. We live in the twenty-first century, but I'm kind of old fashioned like that. Besides, I hated driving long distances and it was at least an hour drive there and another hour back. And what a long friggin' hour getting there was. Tedious. We spent the time listening to the radio and chatting about different bands we'd seen in concert.

Fort Collins is a college town with a lot of rental houses. After a few minutes navigating some side streets off the main stretch, we pulled up to the small cottage house and parked right in front. The streets were narrow here and parallel parking is not my strong suit so I was really glad Mike drove. A woman, probably mid-forties, looked out the window at us.

We got out and walked up the cracking, uneven walkway that meandered through a yard of weeds. Not the nicest house on the block, that's for sure. But then a lot of the rentals here didn't seem to be well maintained. The door opened and Marjorie stepped out onto the small porch, holding the door open. "You must be Liz, come on in," she said through chapped lips, a cigarette hanging out the corner of her mouth. Aside from some seriously deep crows-feet around her eyes, she was actually quite good looking. Her blond hair was neat, her body looked trim and fit. She had shapely legs, soft features, and nice bone structure.

Next to her I felt like a pot-bellied pig. Aside from being plain I'm kind of short and quite frankly, not super skinny. I have a few curves. Of course I'm not what people would consider heavy either.

"The stuff's here in the back room." She led us to a second bedroom across from what seemed to be another bedroom. The room was small and filled with a lot of, well, crap. It was surprising to me anyone could use it for rituals at all it was so cluttered. Then it occurred to me a lot of the stuff seemed to be in boxes.

"You mentioned you were moving?" I asked, feeling my lips contort into a frown.

"Too many memories," she said, giving me a sad smile. She pointed to the altar and a box with a clock, spirit board, and two amulets inside. "Here it is."

Mike looked at the load appraisingly and handed me the box. "Babe, you take the box."

We both looked over the two foot by four foot table. It looked almost like a coffee table, but stood about waist high on me – perfect. It was much better than what I had. The wood, it was real wood, was stained a deep mahogany color and was etched with Daemonic sigils. The legs were sturdy. "Very nice," I said with approval.

Mike nodded at me. "So I guess we're taking it." He smiled at Marjorie and picked up the table as if it was light as a feather and carried it easily out to the car.

I stayed behind with the box tucked under one arm. "Thank you, Marjorie. I'll put these to good use."

Then, amidst the clutter something caught my eye. I noticed several canvases. One painting depicted a dark abyssal scene that looked like a funerary barge with the head of a swan crossing a dark lake. It was done in deep swirls of red and black. I couldn't look away. My fondness for strange, dark art was legendary amongst my friends. My walls at home were a testament to it.

"What's that?" I finally asked.

Her eyes followed mine. "Oh, that's one of my early paintings," Marjorie replied casually. "Do you like it?"

"I love it! It's great!"

She leaned over, picked it up and handed it to me. "It's yours then!"

"Oh no, I couldn't." I felt my cheeks redden. It was nice enough that she was giving me the items she was giving me, but this was too much.

"Really, take it. It would probably end up in storage or in the trash anyway," she assured me with a grin.

But there was something else there. It was almost as if she felt the need to give me more than I came for. Some people are like that, I guess. Generous. Of course she was also moving. Chances are the less she had to move, the better.

I took it. "Thank you."

She smiled and when she did, I caught a glimpse of uneasiness. "No, thank you! They're things I don't have to move now and it will help me move on from this chapter in my life. Thank you Elizabeth and Lucifer Bless."

I stepped out the front door and joined Mike on the curb, handing him the box and the painting, making sure he put the painting where it couldn't get scratched. I gave one last wave to Marjorie, who looked relieved as we pulled from the curb and drove away.

I leaned back in the seat. "Did anything about that seem strange to you?"

Mike shook his head. "Nope. Not unless you count her extensive whip collection. Other than that, no. Last time I moved I gave a ton of crap away so I wouldn't have to move it. Why, did she say something strange?"

I shook my head. "I didn't notice the whips. No, it's just she looked so relieved and was so thankful we took this stuff. So grateful to get it out of her house. I'll probably give the amulets away to friends. I bet Alyssa would like the Satan sigil one," I suggested, knowing Alyssa, one of my closest friends who also happened to be a Satanist, would love it.

"Well," he turned on the right blinker as we pulled up to a stop sign. "If the relationship had a bad breakup, I can understand why she was relieved to get rid of it all. Years ago I shredded everything an ex-girlfriend ever gave me and threw out all the things she bought me. If they'd been worth anything I would have given them to friends who I thought could use them. I don't see this being any different."

"I suppose you're right." I shoved that nagging feeling away with a sigh. "So what about lunch?"

Mike brightened considerably. "I thought you'd never ask!"

After a quick lunch at a *Village Inn*, Mike and I turned back toward home and a quiet Sunday afternoon. Mike's friend, Detective Gary Smith and his wife Lynn were coming over later that night for our occasional game night. Tonight's game was gin rummy. However, I wasn't in the mood for card games. No, something else was bothering me and I had the nagging urge to skry. I looked happily back at my new altar and a sense of discomfort ran through me.

"Remind me to bless all this stuff and make it my own when we get home," I said absently. Not that I expected I'd forget or that Mike really should remind me, but rather to convince that nagging part of myself that I would heed well the advice I was once given by my teacher about used and gifted ritual items. Always bless and clear their energies and *always* make them your own.

Any magician worth his salt never forgets the three C's; clean, clear, and consecrate, my teacher's words rang clear in my thoughts. I leaned back in the passenger seat and stifled a yawn.

Mike turned on the radio to the local college station. They were playing an old *Offspring* tune from the nineties. "Did I ever tell you about the time I pulled over a guy who looked just like Mel Gibson?"

I started laughing because Mike always had the best stories from his patrol days. The detective tales were often more gruesome or scary, but the patrol ones were mildly entertaining. "No," I said.

The rest of the way home he told me about all the celebrity look-alikes he and his other detective friends had pulled over when they were beat cops. The mood lightened and by the time we pulled back into my garage the nagging feeling had left me.

Mike unloaded my newly acquired items from the car and put them into my back bedroom ritual chamber. I immediately inspected the cache then went to work cleaning, clearing and consecrating with some water, salt, incense and a bottle of my infamous consecration oil. A half hour later I emerged only to find Mike had made a spaghetti and garlic bread dinner from what he found in my cupboards.

The rest of night was relatively uneventful. After some intense card playing we called it a night. The house was really cold; frigid in fact. I swear I kept hearing loud booming noises throughout the night. Each time I'd wake up trying to figure out what the noise was. The fifth time a loud crack erupted from the other side of the house I bolted upright and Mike woke up.

"Babe, what's up?" He looked at me bleary eyed, but alert.

"Didn't you hear that?"

He gave me a confused look. "No."

"I thought I heard something. I've been hearing rustling or something, or banging," I whispered, pulling the blanket tighter around me.

Mike leaned down next to the bed and pulled his gun from between the nightstand and the bed. It kind of made me uncomfortable having it in the house, but as long as I didn't touch it, it was all good. He slid out of bed quietly and started creeping toward the door.

"Turn up the heat after you check everything out," I whispered after him.

He nodded and held a finger up to his lips. Then he disappeared into the hallway. I heard him slowly make his way through every room, turning on and off lights. Finally, I heard him pause in the hallway. There were a few ticks from the basement and the heater kicked on. A few seconds later he came back into the bedroom, closed the door and put his gun back into its hiding spot. He slid back into bed.

"Well?" I asked.

He yawned. "All clear, babe. You really need to clean the temple though. It looks like a storage room."

"It's not that bad," I said. "It just has that stuff we picked up earlier in it."

"Yeah, and knocked over incense burners. One of your tarot decks is strewn across the room, and the air altar is tipped over," he said with another yawn as he clicked off the bedside lamp.

I tried to remember it looking that way. It didn't look like that last time I was in there. After my clearing and consecration ritual, I'd put all the new items neatly to the left of the door where Mike had initially stacked them.. The altars had been left untouched. "Well, did you bump into anything and knock it over when you were in there?"

There was a moment of silence and then I felt him shift in the bed. He turned the light back on. "I don't remember knocking anything over. I set the altar and the box of stuff against the wall to the left of the door. That was it. The temple was fine when I was in there this afternoon."

"Well I haven't been in there since earlier this evening when I went in to consecrate and clear the items. But I left it in good order," I told him.

At this point we were both wide awake and sitting up. A chill ran over my arms and neck. Could that have been what all the noise was? Some supernatural force throwing things around my ritual chamber? I got out of bed, grabbing my robe from the chair in the corner. Mike got up, too, following me.

I stepped into the hallway and began walking toward the temple door. There was a heavy feeling in the air. The closer I got to door, the heavier it got. I opened the temple door and clicked on the light. The items we'd picked up still sat against the wall to the left of the door. The other five altars were where they belonged except the Lucifer/Air altar had been tipped over. Similarly, just like Mike had said, all the contents on all the altars had been knocked over or thrown on the floor.

"What the hell?" I moved over to the air altar, up-righting it. I picked up the incense burner and candle from the floor and set them back on the altar where they belonged. Then I set about picking up the tarot deck that had been on the center altar. Once it was picked up, I put the deck back in its bag and stowed it away in the closet that served as my magicians supply pantry. It was very organized.

I went around the room and righted tipped chalices (thankfully empty) and fallen candles. I turned to Mike. "Strange."

He shrugged. "Maybe you just forgot a few things fell over. You know how you sometimes get so fixated on something you don't see past your goal or destination."

I rolled my eyes. "Kind of like how you stare through the television, or your dinner, or me when your mind is on a case?"

He smiled. "Touché."

When I was satisfied everything was back in its rightful place I followed Mike back to bed, but I couldn't help feeling a bit creeped out. The last time I'd seen the contents of altars strewn about was during a haunting investigation I'd done with some friends. The spirit of the house was so angry that we'd tried to exorcise it, that it decided to make a point by knocking over all the items used in the exorcism ritual.

Good gods. What if there was a spirit attached to one or all of the items? And what if my attempt to clear and consecrate them pissed that spirit off? The last thing I needed was another pissed off ghost. Somehow I managed to fall into a fitful sleep.

CHAPTER THREE
MONDAY, JUNE 26

The alarm went off at six. I didn't wake up until seven-thirty and Mike didn't wake up until I shook him. We were both late.

I barely made it into the office by eight-thirty. Luckily no one seemed to notice. I grabbed my coffee cup and hurried to the coffee maker hoping no one had taken the last of the coffee and left it empty as was so common. When I got there, Joyce was there making herself a cup of tea. I breathed a sigh of relief when I saw the freshly brewed pot, completely full, waiting for me. I poured myself a cup, then moved to the counter to add some sugar and cream.

Carrie, our Evangelical co-worker breezed into the break room with her cup of coffee. She reminded me of my aunt Marge, high on Jesus. Much like my aunt, Carrie was able to turn any conversation into a conversation about her Lord and Savior. I was used to it. I usually just smiled and nodded and threw in a well-placed, "Amen" when she was talking (like I did with my aunt, it was easier than disagreeing or trying to discuss spirituality rationally). Really, Carrie was a nice person when you got to know her, and she often made me laugh because she was just so innocent and well-intentioned.

Today, Carrie had something to tell us. She set a copy of her church newsletter on the table in front of us. "You ladies have to read this article. The pagans and devil worshippers are wanting the Air Force to give them a place to worship. Have you ever heard of such a thing?" She poured herself a cup of coffee. "This whole thing and that Satanic Senator a few months back who killed his girlfriend, what is this world coming to? I tell you, we are in the end times. The minions of Satan are growing in numbers and getting ready for Armageddon."

I took a sip of coffee and stifled a laugh. She really was sweet. I did remember the whole Satanic Senator incident. It was because of that particular media frenzy that Mike and I met. But I wasn't telling my co-workers that. As a matter-of-fact I'd managed to keep my co-workers from finding out about my involvement in that whole situation by telling them an old friend had gone missing and that's why I had taken over a week off and how I'd come to meet Mike. No one questioned me. Thank Gods.

"Senator Mitchell didn't kill her," I reminded her. Steve Mitchell hadn't killed his society girlfriend Chloe Brigid Goetic style. No, but a mentally unstable woman, who happened to be a Daemonolatress, had. And she'd been aided by some very misguided followers. "They just thought he did because of the Halloween pictures. Some messed up psychopaths were the ones who killed her."

Carrie looked doubtful. "That's what the liberal media tells us. I don't trust those guys. There's a rise in Satanism, I just know it. Too many things suggest so many people are turning from God."

My co-worker, Joyce, a self-proclaimed Atheist who got annoyed with Carrie easily, chimed in, "They just *make it sound* like there are all sorts of Satanists running around or something like that. As if there's some underground movement we don't know about. Doubtful, Carrie."

I smiled, realizing I probably had a knowing look on my face. "Just because you don't see something doesn't mean it's not there."

Carrie nodded emphatically. "That's right, Liz."

I continued. "Don't get me wrong," I started, thinking of a way to delicately phrase my comments. After all, I knew the truth. Sure - the country wasn't being overrun with Satanists or Daemonolaters or even magi, but there are a lot more of us than the average person knew. "I don't really think we're in the end times, but I do think there are a lot of people with a lot of different, non-Judeo Christian beliefs out there. They're just not overly anxious to share them with everyone."

Both Joyce and Carrie looked at me, saying nothing.

I continued. "Well, like, for example, in some countries they think that because their homosexual population isn't visible that it doesn't exist. They don't want to see it and therefore they can effectively pretend it doesn't exist, when in fact it does."

"I don't know that I like the homosexuals," Carrie said. She made a face. "I just don't understand it. Why would two men or two women want to do that to each other?"

Joyce rolled her eyes and stood. "I have to start on the RyTex invoice order."

I smiled at her. "You want to do lunch later? Tracy's Deli?"

Joyce shook her head. "Nope. Going to lunch with Brian."

"Okay, have fun." I got up, too. "I have some phone calls to make."

"I'll go to Tracy's with you," Carrie offered, the hope clear in her voice. Not a lot of people wanted to have lunch with Carrie because she was a bit too *Holly Hobbie* for most people.

I shrugged. Why the hell not? "Yeah, okay. We'll go at around twelve-thirty."

She smiled brightly. "Sounds great!"

I gave Carrie a pat on the arm as I passed her.

The morning was brutal. Two accounts were avoiding me and thus their bill, and Carrie got cornered by an angry customer who chewed her out over a misprinted order. So when twelve-thirty came we thankfully got the hell out of Dodge.

An uneventful lunch later, we started back to the office. The first mental tug came when Carrie was telling me how she was a youth group counselor at her church and was taking the youngsters camping in August. The second tug came a second later, but not in time.

The red pickup came out of nowhere. As a matter-of-fact I didn't even realize what was happening until it was almost on top of us and smashed into the front end of my car. I think what I remember most was the sound of crunching metal and Carrie screaming. She has a high pitched scream – the kind that makes you want to wet your pants. Ear shattering. I sat completely still until the car stopped moving. The first thing I did was put the car in park and then I look down at myself. I was okay. Then I looked at Carrie. She was fine, too, just startled. Both air bags had deployed and to be honest – I don't remember that part.

People in cars near us were pulling to the side of the road and some guy was tapping on my window asking if we were alright. The guy in the pickup staggered out of his truck, clearly drunk at one o'clock on a Monday. What a douche-nozzle. The police car showed up just as I was about to call our boss. I handed my phone to Carrie and had her call the office. Then I got out of the car and surveyed the front end damage. My car's right front side was pretty messed up and the hood was crumpled.

We waited while the guy who hit us was arrested, and while our cars were towed away, and for the police to take our statements and give us paperwork. *What a crappy day this was turning into,* I decided.

Joyce swung by in her car to pick us up and take us back to the print shop. My car sat on the back of a flatbed, ready to go to an impound yard, waiting for the insurance adjuster to decide if it would be repaired or totaled. Mike was freaking out, calling me every few minutes to make sure I got a case number. To make sure I got the on-scene officer's name and badge number. To make sure I'd gotten all the details I could with regard to the inebriated driver's insurance, which luckily he had. What happened in hours seemed like the whole day. Still, we found ourselves back at the print shop by three.

The rest of the day I couldn't really concentrate. My mind kept going over the accident, then the incident in the temple the night before and how everything was strewn about. When five-thirty rolled around I was done for. Mike showed up at five-forty and we got home at six. This time, he parked his car in my garage. I got out of the car with a heavy sigh, got into the house, disarmed the alarm system and threw my purse onto the dining room table. The house was still cold.

I groaned. It was the friggin' middle of summer and the house was freezing; so cold that we had to turn the heat up the night before. I checked the thermostat in the hall. The temperature was still set at seventy-two degrees, and the temperature in the hallway was registering at sixty-two.

Yet the air conditioning wasn't on, but neither was the heater. Great. I was going to have to call in a professional to figure it out.

Mike followed me. "I know it's been a rough day," he started.

"I think either the air conditioner is broken or the heater is off."

"I turned off the air-conditioner last night and cranked the heat to seventy-two. Just click the switch and it will turn the heater off and the air conditioner on. That should cool the house back down," he said.

"No, it's not hot. The house is freezing." I looked at him, confused. Didn't he feel it?

He looked around the kitchen in a strange way as if he was feeling the cold for the first time. "Did you turn the AC back on this morning?"

"No, that's just it. The thingy is set to heater, it's programmed to seventy-two, and the temperature in the hall is registering at sixty-eight," I explained, pointing at the thermostat. "I think I'm going to open some windows to let heat in. It was eighty-nine today."

"Sounds like the thermostat is broken. Maybe I'll swing by the home store on my way home and grab a new one, and if you'll let me, I'll install it," he suggested.

That meant he was running home to get fresh clothes so he could stay the night. Anymore it seemed either he practically lived at my place or we went to his. We might as well have been living together. "Okay. Sounds good."

He came up behind me and wrapped me in his strong arms. I loved how he did that. Then he leaned over and kissed me on the cheek. "Babe, I know it's been a rough day. Relax. If you want, I'll pick up dinner, you can take a hot bath, and before bed I'll give you a nice massage."

I grinned. I was a very spoiled girl. Sometimes I wondered if it were all a dream. None of my relationships had ever been so good, but only because before Mike, I'd only dated men who were emotionally unavailable or financially inept. Or both. "Okay."

"Don't worry about the car or anything, okay?" He kissed me again.

I took a deep breath. "Okay. But how about I order in Thai for dinner tonight. Sound good?"

"Fair enough. I want my Pad Thai with chicken, none of that tofu shit," he said, walking toward the door.

"Okay, drive safely and I'll see you in a little while. Love you."

He smiled at me, grabbing the garage door opener from the counter. "Love you, too, babe. An hour and a half tops."

With that, he left and I commenced opening a few windows in the living room and my bedroom. It seemed to disperse the cold air. The rest of the house was really cold, too. I went into the guest room and opened the window in there. Then I went into the temple.

A wall of cold smacked me, practically knocking me back. It chilled me to the bone. You would have thought the temple was a freezer. When I entered the room I gasped, feeling overwhelmed and suffocated by the blackness that overtook me. Not only that, but the entire room was torn apart. This time, the four elemental altars had been tipped over and their contents thrown across the room. Sitting neatly on top of the center altar was the deck of tarot cards. Not inside their bag. The tarot bag sat at the edge of the altar.

I drew in a deep breath. Something was going on here and it wasn't physical in nature. It was something supernatural. The skrying mirror on the altar had been placed face down. I lifted it back up and gently placed it back on its stand.

Picking up the tarot deck I shuffled them. Then I pulled three cards. Judgment, The Emperor, and The Hanged Man. I pushed them away and looked into the skrying mirror.

The image came quite unbidden as they sometimes do. Usually I invoke the Daemons and it takes me a few minutes to ascend to the place where I can see things. The mirror usually fogs and clears several times even. This time, it didn't. Instead, clear as day, a man sat looking back at me and I heard a name. Not heard in the traditional sense of hearing mind you, but rather in my mind. My internal voice. The name was Eric Baca. Then, over his face burned the sigil of the Daemon Asmodeus; a Daemon of lust.

Something tugged at my left side. I turned my head toward it, immediately seeing the new altar and the box of items. A darkness hung over it all. Something wasn't right. It made my stomach turn. That's when I realized my teeth were chattering and I was shaking with cold. I breathed out, my breath exhaling a semi-opaque mist.

Startled, I jumped up and left the room behind me and headed straight for the phone.

I dialed Alyssa. The phone rang then made a strange click and I heard breathing.

"Liss?"

"Liz?" Alyssa said, then laughed.

I snorted, "Seriously, girl. I need your help."

"M'kay," she said.

She sounded like there was something in her mouth. "Are you eating?"

"Mm hmm. Yogurt."

"Well stop eating and listen a minute." I heard her laugh again. "Someone gave me some of their unwanted

Daemonolatry items and I think they're haunted, or cursed. I'm not sure which yet."

The other end of the phone went strangely quiet. Then finally she said, "Seriously?"

"Yes, seriously."

"Fuck me. Really?" Alyssa stopped eating.

"Yeah," I paused, not really knowing what to do. "Can you come over later and maybe take a look and get some Daemonic input?"

"Haven't you done that already?" she asked, clearly wondering why I wanted her help. After all, I was quite the talented empath and medium myself. It's just that my abilities were sometimes vague whereas her ability was more forthright.

I paused briefly then said, "I did have a really strange skrying experience, but all I kept getting was a guy's face and name. Besides, my temple is a friggin' freezer. You know how cryptic and strange my abilities can be. It's rare for me to get the same straight forward answers that you seem to get."

It was kind of embarrassing to have to admit that I desperately needed Alyssa's help, but she was the only other talented medium I knew who was close enough to swing by my house. Her ability for ascension and insight was uncanny. Scary even. Of course she was an amazing necromancer, too. She had a relationship with Bune and Euronymous that most Daemonolaters would envy. Besides, I was feeling vulnerable and sometimes a girlfriend could provide a sense of comfort a boyfriend couldn't.

"Oh, okay. Sure. I'll come by. Mind if I bring Gabe?" Her tone was still cheerful, so clearly she didn't mind.

A wave of relief washed over me. "Sure, bring him! He and Mike can hang out."

Alyssa laughed.

"Why is that funny?"

"Gabe is still kind of afraid of Mike. I think it's the whole cop thing," she giggled again. When Mike and Gabe first met there had been some discomfort. Evidently it was still there.

I let out a laugh.

"You've seen the ghost investigators where they find cold spots?" she asked seriously then.

"Yep. You think I have a ghost rather than a curse?"

"Could be that one of the items is haunted," she suggested. "Why do you think it's a curse?"

"A haunting is what I initially thought, too, but then I thought that maybe one or all of the things were cursed since I had such a crappy day today. I was involved in an accident and my car was totaled, and…"

"Holy Satan, Liz! Are you okay?"

"I'm fine. It's just my car that was injured. It was a drunk driver," I explained, then tried to get the conversation back on track. "Or maybe I'm just wishing for a curse rather than a haunt, after all, I'm done with ghosts for the year," I admitted. I'd had more than my fair share of experiences with hauntings, none of them good. "Maybe so, and if that's the case, then you can get rid of it, right?"

"If it agrees to cross over," she said. "Not all hauntings are human spirits though. Sometimes they're entities."

"Now you're freaking me out. Get Gabe and get your butts over here. I'm ordering Thai food!" I didn't bother wondering if Mike would be upset that I'd changed the evening's plans without his input.

She laughed. "Our respective butts are on our way."

We said goodbye after agreeing to a late seven-thirty dinner. After I'd clicked off the phone I immediately dialed

Mike's cell to let him know the plans had changed and to tell him to forget the thermostat replacement for now.

Mike wasn't happy with my assessment of the situation. He was still really jumpy about the more supernatural parts of magick and Daemonolatry after our last encounter with a wayward vengeful ghost.

Alyssa and Gabe arrived a little early and Mike showed up fifteen minutes later. We ate dinner. The house was still freezing. Finally, we couldn't put it off any longer. Alyssa and I looked warily down the hallway at the door.

Being braver than me, Alyssa went first. When she grabbed the door handle she cursed under her breath then said, "The door handle is frozen, don't touch it."

Opening the door, she looked around the room. I hadn't bothered cleaning up the second time. If the ghost or whatever wanted a messy temple, so be it.

Alyssa immediately approached the new items, closed her eyes and drew in a deep breath, touching the altar. "This feels like it does have energy to it, but it seems relatively innocuous." Then she reached into the box and felt the clock. "Same with this clock."

I picked up the spirit board and planchette leaning against the wall and put them on the altar.

"Oh!" Alyssa's eyes lit up. "How pretty." Her hands traced over the intricately carved edges and the wood burnt letters. I could tell she was really giddy over the sigils of Satan and Bune on the board since she was a Satanist who often worked with Bune. Bune was one of those necromancy Daemons necromancers couldn't resist.

"Nice, right? You want it?" I ventured.

"You'd give me this?" She bounced excitedly.

I wasn't nearly that excited about it, even though I did collect spirit boards. Chances are it would sit in my temple closet collecting dust and only get used once a year if that. I had other boards I used more often that were already prepared for Daemonic communication. "Sure. It's yours. Along with that Satan amulet. Only one problem..." I started.

She scrunched her nose and her brows furrowed. She closed her eyes and felt the board then. I could tell she was reaching into it. "The board's cursed," she finished for me.

I lifted an eyebrow. "Not possessed?"

She shook her head. "No. Cursed, sister. Looks like you were right about your run of bad luck."

I opened my mouth to say something, but shut it just as quickly. That was a new one for me. I'd never seen a cursed spirit board.

She picked up the amulets then and actually dropped them. "Those are really cursed, too. Eww." She began shaking out her hands as if she'd accidently touched something really gross with them.

For some reason having cursed items instead of haunted items didn't make me feel any better. "Great. Well that explains why Marjorie looked so guilty and grateful when she handed them over. So do we attempt to un-curse them?"

She nodded. "We can clear it all and then make it our own."

"Wait, what about the painting?" It was leaning against the wall to the right of the new altar.

"Nope, it's fine," she chirped. Leave it to Alyssa to not even allow something like a curse to ruin her good mood. In a way I was kind of jealous I didn't have that same bright, no-one-can-rain-on-my-parade personality she was so well known for.

"So I already cleansed, cleared and consecrated. It obviously didn't work the first time. Should we really bother doing it again?" I gave her a wary look.

She seemed surprised at first. "Wow. Well, let's do it again just to see if two of us is stronger than one of us?"

"Okay, let's do this," I said.

She nodded.

First, I opened the window to let the cold air out and the warm air in. Then I straightened up the temple - again.

We started out with a quick elemental construct and wiped down each of the new items with the blessed water. Then we fumigated the entire space with the banishing incense. And finally, dipping my finger into the *uncrossing oil*, I put my own personal sigil of power on the underside of the altar and the clock. Then I traced the sigil of Leviathan on the backsides of the amulet I was keeping. Alyssa put her own sigil on the back of the spirit board and the Satan amulet.

In theory, this should have worked. But it didn't and it was clear it hadn't when a piercing noise came out of the astral and an invisible force sent both Alyssa and I plummeting backward. I hit the wall with a thud and Alyssa fell on her ass.

We made enough noise to cause Gabe and Mike to rush into the room, both looking bewildered and concerned. "What happened," Mike barked.

Alyssa got up. "We just got our asses kicked."

"The amulets will have to be destroyed," I concluded. With that, I scooped them up, walked wordlessly past Alyssa and the men, and headed straight for the backyard garden with my ritual athame. I was vaguely aware they were following behind me.

"What are you going to do?" Alyssa was right at my heels.

"I'm going to bury them." With that, I fell to my knees in the herb garden and began digging a hole between the sage and lemon balm with my ritual dagger. I carefully avoided the roots of my beautiful lavender plant that I'd grown from a cutting. When the hole was decidedly big enough I dropped the amulets in and covered them with the rich, moist dirt. I looked around at my small herb garden, happy with how it turned out this year. Then I looked back at the cursed burial mound containing the amulets. Hopefully the magickal plants would keep the dark magick contained. I drew a warding symbol in the dirt with my athame. "I commit you to the ground oh wretched beasts!"

I made the blessing of Hecate over the spot then stood up and walked straight back into the house with a satisfied look on my face. Alyssa lingered behind a moment, gazing at the burial mound, and finally followed me into the kitchen. Mike and Gabe had been watching from the back door.

"I have a bad feeling about this, Liz," Alyssa started.

I did, too. But I wasn't ready to admit it. "Well, let's see what happens. You may have to burn the board," I told her.

She shrugged. "Yeah, and sprinkle the ashes over several bodies of running water. We can have the guys start a fire in the pit," she said, motioning toward my backyard.

I shrugged. Reaching into my cupboard, I grabbed a bottle of wine and a cork screw. The cork came out with ease. "Or we could just wait it out."

Alyssa gave me a half-hearted smile. Meanwhile, the men, having no clue what was going on, made a few faces at each other and went back to their card game at the dining room table.

I poured two glasses of wine and handed one to Alyssa. "After this we'll go back in and close that damn ritual."

I downed half the glass of Chardonnay in one gulp.

Oh yeah, it was on. Curse one - Liz and Alyssa zero. I'd never met a curse I couldn't break and the challenge of it consumed me.

That night I had restless dreams; something about a mine shaft and a Daemon. The Daemon wasn't happy with me. Actually, it seemed quite pissed off. I was standing on a glass surface covered in water. There was water everywhere and all around me the horizon was a deep blue with just a hint of light. The Daemon came from the South, humanoid and horned as my Daemons often were when they manifested in my dreams. The Daemon was yelling something that I couldn't understand. I leaned forward (astrally speaking) and tried to hear, but there was too much noise in the foreground. Voices, whispers, clamorous waterfall sounds. I could see the Daemons lips moving. His red eyes pled with me in earnest, but I was helpless to hear him.

CHAPTER FOUR
TUESDAY, JUNE 27

The annoying beep of the alarm clock pulled me out of the dream, and I found myself with the urge to get up and immediately go to the kitchen window to look out at the herb garden. When I got there, cup in hand, I gasped, dropping the cup. It fell to the floor shattering. Mike, protective as he was, flew into the room in a shot.

"What happened?"

I couldn't speak. It was like my voice was gone. I pointed to the herb garden, my eyes wide with fear. All of my previously healthy and green plants were now brown and withered, as if the life had been sucked out of them. Something glinted in the sun from the top of the amulet grave. The soil around the plants appeared untouched.

Mike's eyes followed my gaze and his jaw dropped. "Motherfucker."

Wearing nothing but a pair of Dockers he went outside to the herb garden where I'd buried the amulets. He leaned down and picked something up then came back inside, slamming the amulets on the counter.

"Someone dug them up. They were sitting on top of the ground where you buried them," he said with disbelief.

I still couldn't say anything.

"The entire garden is dead. Give me a plastic bag."

Numb, I opened one of the kitchen drawers and pulled out a plastic bag, handing it to him.

He slipped the amulets inside and closed the baggie, then went to the sink and scrubbed his hands. "There could be some sort of poison in these. Either that or someone is fucking with you again."

I grabbed a broom and started cleaning up the broken cup.

"Liz."

I turned to him.

"This shit has got to stop. I can't go through another incident like we had three months ago," he said. I could see visible concern on his face. It's not like I could help it though. Weird supernatural shit always happened to me. It had been happening since I was a kid. I guess I was used to it. I think he knew I couldn't help it; he just wanted to express his frustration.

"What are you going to do with them?" I finally asked.

"I have a friend at the forensics lab. I'm going to have these tested for prints and poison. There has to be a logical, scientific explanation," he said.

I nodded. "Okay."

There was something about his wavering between skepticism and belief that I found quite endearing. I'd always been a believer. Not a blind believer of course. I have always been one to question my beliefs. But I've never been an outright skeptic either. I'd seen too many things that I couldn't explain away. Curses were one of those things.

After a cup of coffee I retreated to the bedroom to get ready for work. After a quiet drive, Mike dropped me off a few minutes early. There was nothing like arriving to work early to make your day seem long and plodding. The kind of day you can't wait to end. We closed the shop early and Carrie dropped me off at home around five-thirty since Mike had a meeting with the commander that evening. The house was quiet and comfortable. The amulets were with Mike and the spirit board had gone home with Alyssa the night before. The altar and painting were thankfully not cursed, meaning the temperature of the house was back to normal and I wasn't freezing to death. Not to mention the temple was quiet, so I was rather enjoying the lack of cursed items in the house.

It was short lived though. Mike returned home that night with the amulets in tow. He handed them back to me in their baggie. "There has to be a way to get rid of these to where they won't fall into unsuspecting hands. These are dangerous."

I gave him a quizzical look. "Any poison or prints?"

"Neither, but the lab had a fire today. Almost took down the building." He shook his head. "That's some freaky coincidence or something, babe. Enough to make me think we should get rid of them, and that board. It should be burnt. It's still at Alyssa's right? Maybe you should call that Marjorie back and tell her to take the shit back."

That wasn't a bad idea. I went back through my call log, found the number, and dialed it. I got the operator.

"The number you have reached has been disconnected or is no longer in service. Please hang up and try your call again," came the all too familiar tinny voice on the other end of the line.

After I hung up, I called Alyssa to tell her what happened. She had a plan. She and Gabe were going to try a pillar rite to try to infuse the items with positive energy in hopes it would remove the curse. She swung by twenty minutes later and picked up the amulets, taking them home.

That night, the house was comfortable and the darkness that had been hanging over the house that week had dissipated. I felt bad for allowing Alyssa to take the stuff, but to be honest I was thankful for the peace it gave me. I think both Mike and I slept better that night, too. No strange dreams, no mental tugs, no cold spots or visions. All was still.

CHAPTER FIVE
WEDNESDAY, JUNE 28

I woke up at six in the morning to the phone ringing. I instinctively grabbed it as Mike growled into the pillow next to me. "You're calling ten minutes before my alarm clock, it better be good."

She let out an exasperated sigh before saying anything. "It's Alyssa. We did the ritual last night, left it working in the ritual chamber overnight, and I woke up to a broken pipe and a foot of water in the basement. I have the flood guys here pumping it out, but it revealed a foundation crack in my basement floor."

I sat straight up, wide awake. "Damnit. Did you lose anything important?"

"Just my pride as a magician," she quipped. "Look, can you take the day off tomorrow?"

"Sure, why?" I thought for sure she was going to suggest a bonfire or better yet, dropping the items into a mine shaft. The dream from the night before last came flooding back to me.

"There's a psychic fair going on at the county fairgrounds all this week and next. I have a friend there tomorrow who might have some ideas. I'm going to just bring one of the amulets with us and leave the Satan amulet and the board at your place."

"Okay," I agreed. "What time are you picking me up?"

"Nine-thirty. The fair doesn't open until ten," she said. We said goodbye and hung up.

I realized that Mike was staring at me, waiting for an explanation.

"Alyssa's basement flooded. Busted pipe."

He shook his head. "What the hell? This is some freaky, messed up shit, babe."

"I know, but it's not like I can keep this stuff from happening. It just does," I told him.

He placed his hand on my shoulder and gave it a gentle squeeze. "I know. Maybe tonight you should bring the amulets and board here and we'll go stay at my place. That way no one is under the same roof as that stuff."

I nodded in agreement. "We're going to go see someone tomorrow who might be able to help."

"Well call Alyssa back and tell her to drop that shit off here on her way to work this morning, okay?"

I agreed and called Alyssa back, telling her Mike's plan to leave the items in my house and our plans to stay at his place. She sounded relieved and agreed to drop them by.

Finally, with my ritual chamber once again harboring the cursed items, Mike and I headed off to work.

●

Again, Mike picked me up from work and we stopped by my place to pick up a few things. When we got into the house the wall of cold hit me like a brick. Every hair on my body stood on end and my blood ran cold. An overwhelming sense of dread ran through me, but I fought it off. Mike followed me in, looking around as if he expected to see someone there. I went into the bedroom to grab a few changes of clothes (just in case), my makeup bag, and some other necessities. As I emerged from the bedroom I felt a strong mental tug down the hallway.

Still cold and with my eyes filling with unbidden tears, I followed the tug. The nasty energy reverberated from the door, arching outward, pulsating. I could almost see it. It was like a breathing, beating black mass of sludge. My hand went down to the handle of the door and I turned it. With a click the latch sprung open and I went into the room, terrified that someone was in there waiting for me.

Whatever it was – it was watching me. I could feel its eyes. Now, I was fully aware of the tears pouring down my cheeks. My eyes travelled over the items that had become the bane of my existence. The amulets seemed to glow violet. The board just looked like a black mass of swirling fog. At least the altar and clock were okay, and so was the painting, which I had every intention of framing and placing in my hallway. The lone death barge traversed a black sea against the smoky red background. That's how I felt; like I was on a death ship heading into the unknown. Curses had the potential to be a nasty thing if you weren't sure how to break them.

The eyes of the thing turned away from me then.

Mike knocked on the temple door. "Liz, you still in here? What are you doing?"

"Just thinking. Trying to figure it out," I said. My voice sounded distant, hollow. It was like I was standing outside of my body. Not a good thing because that was usually one of the first signs of possession or channeling.

"You know," he started cautiously, which usually meant he was going to say something he didn't think I'd like. "I did some reading today in a few online forums about cursing and they say the more you dwell on the curse, the more it works. You're helping it along. There's a psychological factor to it..."

"It's Eric Baca, we have to find him," I said. But it wasn't me who said it. Let me explain. See, when you're channeling something it can take over your body to use your voice temporarily, leaving you and your own consciousness in a dark place. Whatever had pushed me out and wandered into my body seemed to have some knowledge of what was going on. I tried to ask it who or what it was. It didn't answer, simply surrendered my body back to me and was gone.

I took in a gasp of air.

"What did you see? And who is Eric Baca?"

"He has some connection to Marjorie," I said. I knew that was true. I don't know how, but I knew it. That's the thing about clairsentience. Sometimes you just *know*.

"Good, well, we'll ask around on the online forums and maybe we'll get lucky and find him. Give this stuff back to him or have him take the curse off it," he suggested.

I nodded. That was Mike, always the practical skeptic and one of the things I find most refreshing about him. I followed him out of the temple, through the hallway and back into the kitchen, grabbing my packed bag from the hall floor where I'd dropped it. "I know. There's just something different about this. I mean first I get into a car accident, then when Alyssa took the stuff, her basement floods. There's foundation damage now. I've never encountered a curse this powerful before."

"Well, maybe it's just a coincidence," he said in a hopeful tone that didn't sound convincing. I knew he was just trying to throw a positive spin on things, because he couldn't tell me he didn't believe in curses. Not now. He grabbed my computer and put it into the neoprene case.

"Maybe," I said. Not being as skeptical as him there was no way to convince me this was anything but a curse. I'd felt curses before and whatever was lingering over my house was not a blessing. It was thick and astral sludge filled and it was making me feel sick. It almost felt like an open portal, which was strange. *Maybe it was*, I thought. I shook the thought out of my head.

"Got everything?"

I nodded. With that we armed the security system, locked the door, and left the cursed items and my house behind us for a quiet night at Mike's.

Mike lived in a rustic cabin-style three bedroom house in Golden, nestled in the foothills along the front range of the Rocky Mountains. Golden was an old timey town, home to the Coors Brewery. It almost oozed gold-rush history. Once inside the house I wandered into the living room, breathing in the scent of old house and wood. Okay, so the house wasn't that old. It was probably built in the fifties or sixties.

"Have you ever had this house tested for lead paint?" The thought kind of came from nowhere.

Mike shrugged, carrying my bag to the master bedroom. He left my computer in the living room with me. "No," he called over his shoulder. "But I painted over all the paint in here so if there was, it's buried under a few coats of latex."

I set my laptop on the dining room table.

"Why did you ask that?"

Shrugging I said, "Just a thought I had. Your house is kind of old."

"Sixty-five. Before I moved in I had all the wiring checked, too. Evidently they updated it in the early nineties," he said with a yawn. "TV Dinners okay?"

I nodded. "Sounds good. I'll make them."

So we spent the night in front of the television eating our microwaved dinners and chatting about stuff. I had plans to pick up a rental car the next day so Mike, my co-workers and my friends wouldn't have to keep carting me around.

CHAPTER SIX
THURSDAY, JUNE 29

Alyssa and I arrived just after the metaphysical fair opened its doors. We had swung by my house to grab one of the amulets. The house was still a wall of cold and I blocked my senses off completely to run in and get the amulet without incident. Now at the fair, we wandered around for a few minutes looking at crystals, incense, and tarot decks. It felt good playing hooky. Of course the real reason for our visit loomed.

Most of these people were *white lighters*, also known as *fluffy bunnies*, both phrases some of us who practiced *darker* paths used to describe people who were terrified of anything that might be considered evil – like the religion and magick we practiced. *White lighers* thought those who followed *darker* paths were either immature or too afraid of the light or taking the easy way out. Not becoming enlightened, but rather basking in misery or psychic sludge of some sort. Obviously Alyssa and I (and those like us) disagreed.

We saw ourselves as explorers of what everyone else was afraid of. We also didn't view our paths as *dark and scary.* Love and light and wisdom and enlightenment exist just as much in Daemonolatry and Theistic Satanism and other *dark* Pagan paths as they do in *lighter* more new age paths. We just refused to ignore darkness or run away from it, choosing to explore both the darkness and the light. Personally, I felt it made for a more balanced magician and person overall, but that was just my opinion. I imagined most of these people would have disagreed.

Finally we stepped up to a table of amulets and Alyssa leaned over the table, giving the woman behind it a quick hug. The woman was in her mid-fifties, but still had smooth skin. She was tall, thin, and wore a blue sundress. Her long blonde hair, with a few wisps of gray, fell to her waist in ringlet curls. I was definitely envious of her hair. My hair was so fine it wouldn't hold curls if it was short, let alone medium length like it was now, and most certainly not when it was long.

Alyssa beamed at me. "This is my dear friend, Hera. Hera, this is Liz."

I smiled and nodded politely. "Nice to meet you, Hera." I extended my hand to the older woman and she grasped it firmly with long, thin fingers. I immediately liked her. She had a strong, positive energy around her. The fact that she didn't condemn Alyssa's beliefs or practices as a Satanic Witch spoke volumes in and of itself. Clearly she wasn't one of the biased ones.

Hera smiled warmly at me. "Do you have them with you?" she asked.

I nodded. "We only brought the one," I said, pulling the amulet out of my purse and handing it to her.

Her expression immediately turned grim. She closed her eyes, holding it, then said, "Did these items belong to a violent man? This particular amulet feels heavy, nasty."

My heart sank. Her response merely confirmed that the amulets were imbued with a nasty curse. I nodded.

Then I asked, "Any idea how to constrain them somehow? We've tried making them our own, destroying them and nothing is working."

Alyssa just nodded in agreement. Cursed objects weren't really a specialty for either of us.

Hera tipped her head to the left thoughtfully. "So you have tried making them your own by rituals of your own faith?"

Alyssa and I both nodded and said, "Yeah."

"And you've attempted cleansing, banishing, and re-infusing them within a positive pillar or vortex of energy?"

We both nodded again.

"Buried them?" she tried again.

"Killed my entire garden," I said as an acrid taste filled my mouth.

Alyssa stopped her. "Obviously they've had a strong curse put on them."

"It would be completely irresponsible of us to pass these amulets onto anyone else, or to leave them where they could be found by some unsuspecting victim. Clearly we can't just bury them anywhere and leave them without cursing the very ground they're buried in. It would be harmful to keep them, and we can't seem to destroy them," I said, matter-of-fact. Even if these folks didn't agree with my methods, there was one thing they'd never be able to say about me - that I didn't have ethics or compassion for others. I also took responsibility for my actions. I was the one who agreed to take the amulets. Therefore it was my responsibility to destroy them.

Hera lifted an eyebrow and a small smirk appeared on her lips. "Have you considered tracking down their maker and giving the amulets back to him?"

Alyssa and I looked at each other without words. That was the option I was hoping we wouldn't have to consider just because finding Eric Baca sounded like far more trouble than it was worth. By the look on our faces I'm sure she could tell it wasn't something we were too keen on.

She gave me that look. You know the one – the one your mother gives you when you're being a pain-in-the-ass.

With a resigned sigh I agreed, "Yeah, I guess that's what we'll have to do. We have to find either Marjorie or Eric Baca."

Alyssa nodded, then said thoughtfully, "I wonder how many of these this guy has made and left around for others to find. What if his specialty really is creating cursed objects and leaving them around on purpose, just to hurt other people?"

At that moment you could almost hear the proverbial pin drop. The silence was *that* deafening.

It was Hera's turn to wear a concerned look. "I hope there's no one out there doing that. I wish I had some advice to offer you."

She closed her eyes, still clutching the amulet.

Me and Alyssa exchanged glances, watching Hera do some sort of meditation.

Finally she opened her eyes and handed the amulet back to me. "Unfortunately that's all I can suggest. I can't help you."

I nodded. "Well thank you for taking a look and offering your advice."

She and Alyssa exchanged a few private words and a hug and then Alyssa and I wandered slowly through the merchant tables and finally, found ourselves back at the car.

"So to the rental place?" she asked, probably just to confirm. She already had plans to drop me off at the car rental place and then she and Gabe were doing something.

"Yeah. Then I think I'm going back home, taking the day off. Maybe I'll clean the house and open the windows to warm it up."

She crinkled her forehead. "You staying at Mike's tonight?"

I shrugged. "I don't know. We haven't talked about it yet, but probably. At least until we can find Margie or Eric Baca and give them back their evil."

Alyssa giggled.

•

I drove my rented Toyota to the house and parked it in the driveway. When I got inside it was still freezing so I opened all the windows to let the cold air out and the warm air in. Then I went about dusting, cleaning and putting things away. When I was done, and all that was left was the floor, I decided to take a break and check my email. My computer was still at Mike's, so I used my smart phone.

My mother had sent me another message asking me if I was coming out for Thanksgiving. My parents and my younger brother and his fiancé lived in Arizona. I usually went home every other year for either Thanksgiving or Christmas. I cringed. If I kept avoiding her she'd start calling and leaving messages.

My mom was one of those women who had tried, from the time I was very young, to turn me into a cheerleader-beauty queen. I wasn't even close. There was a reason I lived in another state. Of course after my run in with a murderer a mere three months ago, and after ending up in the hospital, I did call my parents to tell them I'd had a little accident just in case they somehow found out. No, I wasn't truthful about it. But ever since then my mom had begun using the incident to try to convince me to move back to Arizona. She had plenty of eligible men she wanted to introduce me to. After all, I was already thirty and an old maid.

So to get her to quit trying to set me up with either their neighbor's son, Bastian Marlow, or some guy named Eric Peters, I finally broke down and told her I was seeing Mike. Under threat of her and my dad coming for a visit, I had somewhat, non-committedly, suggested that maybe Mike and I would both come out for Thanksgiving. Mike didn't know about it yet. I made a mental note to send her an e-mail later telling her I'd have to talk to Mike, and then I made a mental note to actually mention it to *him*. With an exasperated sigh I moved on to the rest of my inbox. Nothing important seemed to be going on in cyberspace. With nothing left to keep me from the inevitable, I decided to vacuum.

Just as I'd finished up the bedrooms and started on the living room I felt a strange nagging sensation like the ones I often felt when the Daemonic Divine was trying to get my attention. This naturally caused me to stop my menial task of vacuuming.

Something wasn't right.

The light was all wrong. I looked down at the clock noting it was only 3:30 in the afternoon. I looked out the window. A sudden onset of panic rose in me when I saw the sky. It was black and it seemed to be churning. I felt a cold chill. Holy Daemons. I'd only seen the sky get that black in the middle of the day one other time in my life. It was when I was visiting relatives in Kansas one summer. All of us kids were herded into the root cellar that day. But this was ridiculous. This was Colorado, right along the front range. Tornados didn't hit this far west, did they?

The hail started first. I could hear it falling outside. It sounded like someone dropped about a thousand of those small, hard, bouncy balls. I wondered for a second if my rental car parked in the driveway would be okay until a voice in my head told me sternly, "*Find shelter. Get below!*"

For some reason I grabbed my coat, put it on and grabbed my purse from the hook and headed into the basement. That's when I heard it - something that sounded like a train. Not a train whistle or horn, just the sound a train made going over the tracks. That loud *thunk-thunk-thunk-thunk-thunk-thunk*.

A loud crack caused me to drop and I felt something push me under the staircase, like a strong wind. Covering my head I crouched there, terrified, trying my best not to scream. Loud snapping and crunching noises made the entire world sound like it was coming to an end. The roar was deafening. This was it. Armageddon had finally come and I was a goner.

"Euronymous bless and keep me this day of my death," I heard myself whisper. I guess there really weren't any Atheists in foxholes.

But the calamity and noise began subsiding and from behind me there was a bright light, a cool rush of air and then I felt water dripping. I turned around and looked up and out the doorway of the small space beneath the stairs to see the gray sky above as the rain came down without mercy into what used to be my house; the front half of it anyway. The sound of sirens in the distance brought me out of the trance-like-state I was in and back to reality.

Carefully I climbed out from under the staircase and kind of moved to the center of what used to be my small basement. None of my plastic storage totes were worse for the wear and it was likely they'd hold up to the water. I was still alive and I hadn't lost everything - just a huge chunk of my house. I looked up and around. The entire kitchen, dining room, and living room were gone. However, all the bedrooms of the house were still standing, which meant the cursed items were still intact in the ritual chamber. How that had happened was beyond me. Usually houses were obliterated, like my neighbor's. His house was gone and all the others around us looked a bit damaged. From where I stood I could see shingles hanging off of neighbor's roofs, gutters hanging off houses, tree branches snapped, and people's lawn furniture strewn about. It was quite a mess.

"Miss, stay there and watch for any exposed power or gas lines. I'll get a ladder so we can get you out," came a man's voice in front of me. I looked up to see one of my neighbors from down the block standing there. "You alright?"

I just nodded, still in shock. My rental car was nowhere to be seen from where I was standing, and to my right I heard water trickling. I turned to see a busted pipe spilling water onto the ground. Instinctively I walked over to the water main valve and shut it off. There was a sudden hush as the trickle of water died.

"Was anyone else in the house with you?" came the man's voice again.

"No," I said. For the first time I really looked at him. He was bald, about fifty, and wearing jeans and button down shirt with tennis shoes. My mind began to race, wondering what I could salvage immediately and whether or not my insurance policy covered tornado damage. The sound of sirens was closer now, almost on top of us.

Another man brought the ladder and after a few minutes I'd managed to climb out of the hole and look at my house from the sidewalk. It looked like we were standing in a junkyard.

It wasn't long before the news media arrived to film the aftermath of the tornado that, evidently, had merely touched down on my house, obliterated the neighbor's, and then retracted back into the sky. Luckily the neighbor and his wife were both at work when it happened and they didn't have pets or children.

I realized I had my phone in my purse. I was thankful I grabbed it. I turned on the phone to see I'd missed a few calls from Mike, one from Alyssa, another from Lynn Smith, and one from my mother. My weather application had a red exclamation point on it. I opened it to reveal the tornado warning. It figured. I was infamously plugged into the world and always had the news on and yet today of all days I'd chosen to keep the television off and the phone silent in my purse. I dialed Mike's number.

I rang only once before he picked it up. "Liz, you okay?"

"I'm fine," I said, realizing my voice sounded lifeless. "The rental car is upside down on the neighbor's front lawn and I no longer have a house, but I'm still alive."

The reality of the situation hit me like a ton of bricks. I felt the tears beginning to seep out of the corner of my eyes even though I was doing everything I could to stop them.

I heard his audible sigh of relief. "I'm stuck in traffic. Lynn Smith is on the way there right now with the pickup, I'll be there in a little while. We'll rent a moving truck and get whatever we can salvage moved over to my place for the foreseeable future."

"How did you know?" I asked, sniffing back the flood of tears threatening to overflow my emotional defenses despite my resolve to stay calm.

"You mean aside from the news?"

"Yeah."

"Let's just say a little divine helper gave me a heads up, but we'll talk about that later. Are you sure you're not hurt?"

"Yeah," I repeated. Have you ever felt hopeless? That's how I felt in that moment. Hopeless.

"Alright, I'll see you in a little bit. Hang in there. Love you."

Right at that second that's exactly what I needed to hear. That *Love You* was like a huge psychic hug. "I love you, too." I hung up the phone with a sorrowful sigh.

I felt a light tug on my sleeve then. There stood old Mrs. Lawrence, my eighty-four-year-old neighbor from two doors down, with a cup of coffee in hand. "Here, dear, you drink this."

I took the cup gratefully. "Thank you."

She patted my arm and turned back toward her house. I took a sip of the coffee then set about calling my insurance agent. I even took a few pictures on my phone and forwarded them to her. I decided not to call my mother back. I hoped Mike hadn't called her, but it was completely possible she'd just called to see if I got her email. She was notorious for doing that; sending email then calling to make sure I got it, which kind of defeated the purpose of sending the email to begin with.

After the firemen had completely inspected my house and the police had effectively kept the media away from me, I was approached by a few of the firemen. "It seems you turned off the water already?"

I nodded. "I was in the basement under the stairs when it hit, so once it was over I was able to turn off the water main," I explained.

"Oh good," the guy said. "Well, we were able to get the gas to the house shut off. Could have been a lot worse if you had the furnace on or a stove or something. If you're going to go in there and take stuff out I suggest being very careful. None of the structure that's still standing looks like it will fall into the basement there, but it could be hard to navigate. There could be sharp edges on the wood and all that. We'll be here for a little while to tape this off from the street. Maybe keep the neighbors, media, and kids off the property – for safety."

I tried to smile, but I couldn't. "Thanks."

"Do you have a place to go and do you need some help salvaging a few things?" another one asked. "We can contact some help agencies for you…"

"No, I have friends and my boyfriend on their way right now to help me get some stuff and take it over to my boyfriend's. I'll be staying there," I said, feeling numb.

The firefighters went back to their business.

I'm pretty sure Lynn Smith arrived first. Lynn, the wife of Mike's friend Gary, was blonde, perky and surprisingly intelligent. She was a university professor who taught cultural anthropology. There was nothing stupid or metaphorically blonde about her. Of course her perkiness was a stark contrast to my usually mellow, somewhat cynical some would say, demeanor, and quite frankly it sometimes annoyed the hell out of me. Today, however, she was subdued. After telling the police officers around the perimeter of the flagged area who she was, they let her through and she made her way to me, her eyes wide as saucers as she looked at my house. Or rather what was left of it.

"Oh my God, Liz!" An overwhelming surge of emotion crossed her face and I actually felt it burst out of her. She threw her arms around me. "I'm so glad you're alive. We could have lost you!"

I gave her a weak smile and hugged her back, trying to balance the cup of coffee aloft in my left hand. Surprisingly I didn't break down and start crying. I was too numb.

"Gary and Mike and a few of the guys who are off today are coming over to help load up the truck. I guess one of them is picking up a moving truck," she said, her eyes fixated on the disaster that was my living room.

"Okay," I said. I wasn't sure what else to say and neither did Lynn. Luckily my phone rang, breaking the awkward silence. It was my insurance agent. She said she had a claims adjuster on the way. That was good news. Another bit of good news came five minutes later when the rain finally stopped.

"I hope I can salvage what little of my life is left," I said aloud to no one in particular.

Lynn didn't say anything further. I imagine it had to be uncomfortable for her. After all, what can one really say when a friend loses an entire house in a matter of minutes? Nothing she could have said would have helped and the fact that she was there, just standing next to me, meant more than words anyway.

It took a few hours, but with the help of Mike, Lynn, Gary, Alyssa, Gabe, and a few off duty detectives from the Denver PD, we had what was salvageable from my house in a moving van on its way to Mike's. Luckily many of my books, the contents of three bedrooms, and most everything in plastic totes from the basement was saved. It all fit into the moving van without any problems. If one could measure one's life in boxes, mine amounted to very little.

Everything went in the moving van including the altar, clock and painting. The only exceptions were the cursed amulets and the spirit board. I decidedly sent those with Alyssa and Gabe who had a plan to hide them on Gabe's uncle's property somewhere up in the mountains for the time being. That way we could, hopefully, keep them out of unsuspecting hands and as far away from us as possible for the foreseeable future. I was terrified though; terrified that Alyssa and Gabe would die in a fiery car crash after they slid off the road and over a mountainous cliff. What can I say? I have an active imagination. But alas, Gabe had a plan.

He pulled out the black bag with a sigil of Cthulhu on it. It was about as big as a pillow case. As a matter of fact, I think it was a pillow case and I'm pretty sure the sigil was made out of fabric paint. I could feel myself smirking.

"Don't be a naysayer," he said sternly.

"Okay, so what's up with the bag?" I asked.

Alyssa and Mike both shook their heads and stayed out of it.

"The bag is what I call a diffuser. I've basically imbued it with the power to contain any magickal item for at least a few hours. We can get up to my uncle's property in forty-five minutes tops." He looked at the items with a wary sigh. Clearly he wasn't as confident in his cotton diffuser bag as he thought.

"Alright. You both have your cell phones?" I asked, acutely aware I sounded like someone's mother.

"Check," Alyssa beamed.

"They're charged?" I prodded.

Alyssa put her arm around me. "Would you stop being such a worrier? Gabe and I can handle ourselves. We'll be careful. Once we've ditched these suckers I'll call you to let you know we're okay."

I nodded. "Promise?"

"Promise," she agreed. "I'm more worried about you than me. Get some rest."

With that, Gabe scooped up the cursed items and stuffed them in the bag. Quick as a flash, he and Alyssa got into the car and drove off leaving me there with Mike. Everyone else had already gone ahead to Mike's with my meager possessions. We climbed into Mike's car and headed to his place. My new home-sweet-home until I figured out what I was going to do.

CHAPTER SEVEN
FRIDAY, JUNE 30

As if things weren't bad enough, I was pretty sure my boyfriend was questioning my sanity. Or it seemed that way.

"Are you sure the guy's name was Eric Baca? Let's do another skrying just to make sure," Mike said. He was using that detective tone with me; a sure way to make me mad in a hurry.

I let out an exasperated sigh and turned toward his spare bedroom to get the skrying mirror and candles. "Fine."

When I got back, Alyssa sat quietly and Mike gave me his *sorry* look. Well if he wasn't going to man-up and say it, I wasn't going to forgive him. Not immediately anyway.

The morning sun cascaded through the windows, so I set the skrying mirror on the table and went to shut the drapes. I'd already called in to work and told my boss I wasn't coming in. Lucky for me I still had over a month's vacation time just sitting there, not including past years where I hadn't taken any vacation time at all. Mike and Alyssa had taken the day off, too, using the valid excuse that

I had just lost my home and needed both of them. That was close to the truth.

I sat down in front of the coffee table and lit the candles. I searched the reflective depth of the mirror. Closing my eyes, I drew in a deep breath, relaxing myself and focusing. Slowly I opened my eyes and gazed into the mirror. It began to cloud, the blackness fading into a fog. Then it cleared and standing there was a man with black hair. *Eric Baca* my internal voice whispered. I could have just closed the session right there. Instead, I decided to dig deeper. I'd go beyond the mirror, ascending to the Daemonic plane to speak with any Divine Intelligence who offered up more information.

Surprisingly it only took me a few seconds to connect. I felt the Daemon inside my head. My every pore palpitated as the energy ran through me. It was like being plugged into a low level energy source. Not enough to kill you, but certainly enough to cause exhaustion and stress on the physical body. *Who are you?* I mentally asked the Daemon who presented himself.

I saw the Daemon's face. It was male; its face thin, with sunken cheeks framed by soft black locks of hair. The eyes were the most striking of course. With Daemons that always seemed to be the case. Its infinite eyes glowed crimson and when I looked into them I felt a staggering, overwhelming lust run through me. Heat radiated between my thighs. *Asmodeus*, I thought in recognition. The Daemon of lust.

Unbeknownst to a lot of people, Asmodeus and I had a history. The rapport was good.

"Eric Baca," the Daemon told me as if I was being difficult. Perhaps I was.

"He can remove the curse?"

"Find him. It's urgent." The Daemon wasn't his usually jovial self. He was dead serious. Even the playful glint in his eyes that I had become accustomed to during previous encounters was gone.

"I'll find him," I said.

"Good, now go." Yeah, it was that blunt.

I felt the Daemon detach. It was like being unplugged from the current. Taking my time, I slowly brought myself out of the connection, yawned, and opened my eyes. Alyssa was sitting across from me with a pad of paper and Mike was pale as a ghost. He looked scared.

"Was I channeling?" I winced.

Alyssa nodded. "Yeah. You even did the scary Daemon voice. I have it recorded, want to hear?"

I looked at the coffee table to see Alyssa's phone sitting there. It must have also been a voice recorder.

She hit play.

From the small, tinny speakers I heard my own voice, but not. It sounded awful. Rough. Scary. "Find Eric Baca. He shall die. Die. The curse kills. Do not surrender," I, channeling the Daemon, said.

Funny – I didn't remember that part. The audio file ended.

"Lovely." I looked over at Mike. He looked at me with uncertainty and began looking behind me. "You know that wasn't me, right?"

"Yeah, I kinda figured." His eyes darted toward the hallway.

"What are you looking at?"

"I'm looking for *it*," he said.

Alyssa was strangely quiet.

"It?" I looked at Alyssa, my eyes pleading for an explanation.

"Remember when we were in our early twenties and we did that séance at Mary Stetson's house?" she asked.

"Oh," I said. She didn't have to say anymore. I remembered it well. All the people except me and Alyssa had run out of the room screaming that night. Evidently, and I'm only going by what I've been told, a dark figure merged with me and began talking through me. And when it was done, it separated from my body and left, vanishing down a dark hallway. It had been Asmodeus that time, too.

"Asmodeus?" Alyssa clarified.

I nodded. "I guess he has the same MO."

"Yeah, well now I've got creepy shit running around my house." Mike frowned. Then he got up, pulled me to my feet and wrapped his arms around me. "This stuff needs to stop happening."

"Because it freaks you out?" I asked.

"Precisely."

Alyssa chuckled.

Then something occurred to me. I pulled back from his embrace and looked into his dark eyes. "You told me on the phone yesterday after the tornado that you were given a Daemonic heads up. What was that all about?"

"I knew you'd eventually bring that up."

"What happened," Alyssa asked.

Mike took a deep breath. "I was at the station and this guy I've never seen before walked into my office and said 'You need to check on your girlfriend. There was a tornado and her house was destroyed.' Then he walked out of my office. I tried to go after him but I couldn't find him. He wasn't anyone I've ever seen there before. He had shoulder length black hair, tall, thin, dark eyes. It was like he vanished, but I immediately checked the news and sure enough there was the report. So I started calling you, left messages, got in the car and headed in your direction."

"That sounds like Asmodeus," I said offhandedly. "When I was ascending with him just now he kept telling me to find Eric Baca. I don't remember that stuff on your voice recording."

"I don't get the whole Asmodeus connection with you. It's not like he's your patron or anything," Alyssa said, shrugging. Then her eyes got big and started toward the kitchen like a dog who had just been distracted by a squirrel. "I bet the coffee's done!"

I laughed and took Mike by the hand. We followed her into the kitchen. Mike still gave a backward glance as if he expected Asmodeus to materialize out of thin air.

"Where do we even start finding this Eric Baca? I've asked everyone I know who practices Daemonolatry and no one knows who he is." Alyssa said, pouring two cups of coffee and handing me one.

"No kidding! I know. I checked The Order's membership roster on the computer earlier and he's not on it. Everyone online uses a pseudonym, obviously." I said, defeated. We sat down at the kitchen table with our coffee.

Mike poured himself a cup. "Well, I know where to start."

We both turned toward him.

"Miss Margie Ellis, if you recall, had an impressive collection of single tail whips and floggers. My guess is she might be into some kinky stuff."

Alyssa's eyes lit up. "Are you sure?"

"That's right," I said, remembering Mike's comment the day we drove back from Fort Collins.

"Oh, I'm sure. She had different colors, sizes, and I'm pretty sure they were made out of varying materials." He took a sip of coffee with a satisfied look on his face.

I looked at Alyssa with what I'm sure was a proud smile. "That's why he's the detective."

Mike chuckled.

Alyssa pointed at me. "My friend Megan works at *Leather and Lace*. They have a whole range of fetish gear."

"Whips you mean?" I asked. Yeah, I was a bit naïve about the whole fetish thing. When it came to sex I was rather monogamous and not all that adventurous. My idea of kinky was trying on different lingerie, which was stupid since it was going to end up on the floor almost immediately anyway.

She nodded. "I'll call her."

"Good, is she working now?" Mike asked, sitting down at the table with us.

"Yep." Alyssa already had her phone out and the phone dialed. She put the phone on speaker and set it on the table between all of us.

"*Leather and Lace*, this is Meg."

"Meg – it's Alyssa. You guys sell lots of whips there?"

"Hey Liss! Um, yeah, you and Gabe doing some exploration?"

Alyssa blushed. "No actually. Um, actually I'm looking for someone who might be one of your customers."

"Oh?" Megan paused for a second then said, "Yeah, they're twelve-ninety five each. Sorry, customers. Who you looking for?"

"An old friend's boyfriend. Her name Marjorie Ellis and his name is Eric Baca. I have something of his that I need to return to him." At least she wasn't lying.

"Baca, that sounds really familiar. Hold on a sec." We could hear her take the phone away from her face to address a co-worker. "Dan, Eric Baca – I've heard that name before. How can I find him?"

We heard a man say something in the background but it wasn't audible.

"Oh, okay. Um, he's a guy who makes specialized bdsm gear for like Satanists and stuff, right?" Megan asked as if Alyssa should know.

Mike nodded at Alyssa as a cue that she should act like she knew.

Alyssa got the cue. "Yeah, that's him."

"Okay, so like I don't know how to get ahold of him, but I know who you can talk to. You have to talk to Reg Mathers. I don't have his number though and he'd probably be pissed if you looked him up and found out I told you where he was. He's a very private guy. But I can tell you where he hangs."

"Great! Where?" Alyssa maintained her bright demeanor as always.

"*Kat 09* off of I-25 and twenty-third," Megan told her.

Alyssa's facial expression turned amused for a second. "The BDSM club?"

"That's the one. The only problem is they won't let you in without a partner and unless you're playing the part. How bad you want to find this Baca guy?"

"I really want to give him his stuff back," she said. Then she shrugged at us.

"Well come in with Gabe and I can deck you guys out so you at least look the part, though it sounds like a lot of work just to give someone their stuff back. I'd sell it online." Megan kind of laughed.

Alyssa snickered. "I wish it were that easy. But okay, I'll be coming in with some friends. We'll make it a double-duty night out. Sounds our kind of date-night adventure."

"That's the spirit! You'll like *Kat 09*, it's really cool. Great people. So see you tonight to get you outfitted before tomorrow night? Kay? Saturday is public couples play, no private events at the club and Reg is sure to be there!"

Megan chirped. Then she added with regret, "I'm working though so I won't be there, otherwise I'd introduce you. But I'm sure someone there will point him out or he'll introduce himself. He always chats with newbies."

"Oh, okay," Alyssa agreed. Then they said goodbye and she hung up. She looked at Mike, clearly waiting for his approval.

He gave it. "Looks like we're in business. We'll go talk to this Reg guy, find Eric Baca and meet with him to give him his stuff back."

Let me be frank for a moment. I was the only one concerned about the whole idea of going to a BDSM club. It didn't seem to bother Alyssa or Mike though, so I decided to keep my concerns to myself.

●

Thirty-years-old and this was the first time I'd ever been in a sex shop. Most people had at least gone into one on a dare. Somehow, despite the fact that I went to a party college and despite the fact that I had friends far more adventurous than me, the experience of a sex store had eluded me until now.

Alyssa greeted her friend, Megan, and they exchanged some conversation then Megan went back to helping a customer and Alyssa made her way into the racks of fetish clothing.

The air smelled heavy of leather and chemicals; probably from the shelves full of sex toys on one side of the store and racks full of latex and leather on the other. Mike wandered among the racks of women's lacy things eyeing what he liked and looking at me as if gauging how it would look. I shot him my *don't press your luck* look and scowled at the rack of corsets in front of me.

Alyssa, in usual Alyssa fashion, pulled items off the racks and held them up to herself in front of a full length mirror. She was leggier and taller than me. With her body I imagined she could wear just about anything and it would look good. I, on the other hand, being short and somewhat frumpy, would not only have to buy everything in size large, but also something flattering to my shorter stature.

Alyssa loaded up one arm with outfits then moved to shoes. I heard her squeal in delight before she cried out, "Oh my Infernal Gods, Liz, these shoes are *so* you!"

Her hand shot up from behind a rack holding a pair of shapely black stilettos in a size eight. My jaw dropped. I hurried over to her. "I can't walk in those. I'll trip and dive face first into the ground."

She shrugged, handing the shoes to me. "Just practice a little before we go. Besides, you'll be wearing this." With a flourish she produced one black latex mini-dress from the armful of clothing draped over her left forearm. "Those shoes are going to totally complete this outfit. Those are hot with *this*."

I must have looked mortified because she laughed at me and shook her head.

Before I could regain enough composure to respond, I heard Mike come up behind me. "See, babe, Alyssa's got you covered, though not by much." He reached out and felt the dress. "What is that?"

"That's latex," Alyssa said. "You'll have to use talc powder or cornstarch to get into it and rinse it with water afterward, but it feels so awesome against your skin. Oh, and you can really only wear it for an hour or so before you'll need to re-powder, but it's totally worth it."

I opened my mouth to speak but nothing came out.

"Kind of seems like a pain in the ass..." Mike started.

"But it's really hot, trust me. We'll get some stuff to shine it and she'll look the part." Alyssa seemed really pleased with herself.

I wasn't so thrilled.

Alyssa had enough empathy to notice this. "I promise it's going to be super sexy. Besides, how often do we get to do a double-date fetish night?"

I felt the heat creep up my neck, into my cheeks. I was sure my face was a deep crimson with embarrassment. That's what happens when you're raised with the notion that sex is dirty and evil. There just weren't words, but I didn't protest. In retrospect I probably should have said something, but I kept my mouth shut.

I followed Mike around the store with Alyssa's friend, Megan, leading us from rack to shelf until he found a pair of black leather pants, some black boots, and a black silk shirt he could live with. We completed the shopping excursion with a riding crop for Mike and a leather collar and wrist bands for me. Aside from the occasional yes or no to Mike's selections, Alyssa kept herself busy shopping for her and Gabe. After an hour and several hundred dollars the three of us emerged from *Leather and Lace* outfitted for a night at *Kat 09*.

When Saturday night rolled around, I was really wishing I'd opened my mouth and said something the night before.

CHAPTER EIGHT
SATURDAY, JULY 1

I looked down at myself. The latex dress was not only risqué, but the collar and wrist bands were just too much. The black stilettos were already killing my feet. I pulled my hair back into a neat, slick bun, and figured my makeup was just enough to convince anyone that we really were *Kat 09* material. Alyssa was right – the outfit *did* look good on me. I could hear Mike in the other room mumbling something that sounded like *Fuckin' seriously?*

I took a deep breath and pulled open the bathroom door, stepping into the bedroom.

Mike looked up and his eyes went wide. "Wow, babe, that's pretty hot."

I put my hands on my hips and said sharply, "I had to powder myself up to get into the panties and this dress. These heels are murder, so this better be worth it. Or as Alyssa said, there's no way we're going to get into *Kat 09* without the proper attire."

Mike chuckled. "She's right."

I noticed he was already dressed in the leather pants, black silk shirt, and heavy black boots he'd decided on at the shop, at Alyssa and Megan's suggestion. He had the riding crop in his back pocket. An amused grin crossed over his lips.

"What?" I was rethinking the latex g-string panties and I was pretty sure at that point Mike was, too, but not in the same way.

"This could be fun." His smile broadened. "You'll have to be a good girl or I'll give you a spanking."

My cheeks flushed red. Good Gods! You'd have thought I was Catholic or something. "Ha ha."

"You think I'm kidding," he said, eyeing the outfit. "Just how far does that dress hike up when you sit down?"

I looked down at the dress and ran my hands over it. I had no idea if I could sit down in it or not. I did know this though – the latex felt pretty good against my skin. It was an interesting sensation. I just hoped no one I knew saw me in it.

"Come here," he said, pointing right in front of him with the crop.

My cheeks burned even more. "Mike…"

"Come here," he said more firmly.

A shiver of excitement ran through me and I carefully made my way to him as fast as I could in those awful stilettos.

"Damn that's hot," he whispered, looking me up and down.

"Alyssa is going to be here in a while," I reminded him, looking at the alarm clock on the bedside table.

"We can play a little until she gets here. Just bend over for a minute and put your hands on the bed," he said huskily.

"Michael!"

He took me by the arm gently, but firmly, and turned me toward the bed, then gently pushed my shoulders down. His hand went to my bottom and began rubbing. It felt awesome against the latex. I felt a familiar longing between my thighs. He playfully smacked my rear with his hand then rubbed me some more.

I could hear his breathing getting heavier. He carefully lifted my dress, exposing my bare bottom, then set to work playfully swatting me with the crop. I moaned softly. I don't know why, but it felt good and a familiar tingling started in my lower abdomen and shuddered between my thighs.

His hands moved over my bare flesh. "Stand up," he ordered.

I stood, feeling my nipples go hard.

He wrapped his arms around me and his lips and tongue explored my neck and ear. "No sense tonight needs to be all about cursed objects, right?"

His hands began exploring my body over the latex sending shooting pleasure through me. I didn't speak, just closed my eyes, leaned against him and enjoyed his touch. He kissed my neck again, driving me wild. I wanted to rip off the clothes and pull him onto the bed for a rather passionate romp. But I refrained. Good thing, too.

The doorbell rang and I instinctively pulled my latex dress back down over my assets.

"Alyssa," we both said.

Mike took a deep breath, laughed and looked down, "You better get that."

My eyes followed his and I realized why. "Will do."

I tried to walk as confidently as I could in the stilettos. I'd been practicing. It wasn't easy and it made my calves hurt. Mike all but ran into the bathroom to take care of his, well, you know.

When I opened the front door, Alyssa was decked out in an even kinkier outfit than mine consisting of leather pants and a leather corset. With her confidence she could pull it off.

"Lookin' hot, Liz!" She stepped into the house leading her boyfriend Gabe on a chain. Gabe looked like leather boy. It was actually kind of sexy. He had nice chest, solid biceps and nice rear view. All attributes his *slave* outfit played up.

"Hey Liz," Gabe said. He smiled at me, not seeming to mind playing Alyssa's sub-boy for the night. "So are you ready for your first night as a submissive?"

I nodded, holding up my wrists so they could see the metal rings on the wrist bands.

Alyssa's hand reached out to grab my wrist. "Oh, you got the cool fuzzy comfy ones."

"Yeah. Mike insisted I be comfortable if I have to wear leather wrist bands."

"So how does Master Michael look?" She smiled. She was enjoying this way too much.

I wondered then just how much about the whole BDSM scene Alyssa really knew. She seemed more experienced than she let on. "He looks pretty hot with that riding crop." I felt myself flush.

She smiled at me. "It's a kick, right? Nothing like a little role playing to spice up things in the bedroom." She gave me a wink.

I blushed and turned away just as Mike walked into the room looking like a Greek God. His silk shirt was open just enough so I could make out his well chiseled chest. He was really in shape. "Alyssa, Gabe, how are you guys?"

"Ready to go!" Alyssa sang cheerfully.

"You do this often?" I asked.

Alyssa laughed. "I've never been to a BDSM club, but I'm no stranger to a little exploration in the bedroom."

She gave Gabe a long come-hither sideways glance and he returned it.

Mike cleared his throat.

Alyssa turned her attention back to everyone. "Okay, so remember – submissives – you have to do what we say and remember to be meek or we'll have to openly punish you. Tonight's safe word is *red*. The club evidently has their own safe word, too. It might be *red* as well since that seems to be the standard."

My eyes went wide. "We're going to need a safe word?"

Mike said nothing, just nodded.

Alyssa put a reassuring hand on my shoulder. "Just in case. Megan said *Kat 09* is a bit of a playground. They don't just sit around and talk dungeons or have a drink. People actually do the whole Dom/sub thing and Doms show their subs off and publicly humiliate them, spank them, or whatever. If we need to convince anyone we are what we say we are, that might mean openly giving one of you a spanking." She looked at Gabe when she said that.

I suppose it's the fact that I'm a bit prudish that I started to bulk. "Maybe it would just be easier to track this Reg guy down at his home and question him there. Or maybe you and Mike go and leave Gabe and I here."

Mike leaned over me and whispered in my ear, "Come on, babe. Don't be a chicken. Alyssa and I will ask the questions, you two just keep quiet and do what you're told. We'll only be there an hour tops."

Gabe just smiled, saying nothing.

"We should go," Alyssa finally said.

Denver has all kinds of strange little bistros, shops, and clubs hidden in some of the most innocuous places. Places you'd never consider looking. *Kat 09*, as in Cat O'Nine Tails, was no different. It was located in a building right in the middle of one of the upcoming neighborhoods just a few blocks west of I-25. There were bouncers at the door. If you were alone, you couldn't get in. A sign in the window next to one of them said, *Couples Only.* Fear and excitement raced through me as Alyssa looked for a parking spot. Mike's hand ran teasingly along my inner thigh, by the knee. When I sat, the dress was incredibly short. Had I not been wearing panties, everyone would have seen, well, everything.

She finally pulled into a parking spot close by and I held onto Mike's arm as he helped me out of the car. I pulled down on the skirt of my dress to make sure nothing was showing. "Come on little slave girl," he said jokingly and gave me a wink.

I followed, a little behind him, holding onto his arm to steady myself. The arches of my feet were already starting to really hurt. Heels weren't my thing.

Alyssa and Mike walked confidently up to the rope leading Gabe and me. The two huge men at the door eyed us, giving us the once over. With a nod to his friend, the one working the rope unhooked it and let us pass into the dark doorway beyond. Alyssa and Mike paid the cover charges (twenty per person), we all signed waivers and liability forms saying we'd read the club rules. Finally, we were allowed to step into the dark cavernous club beyond. Evidently the club safe word was also *'red'* and there were men in orange vests called *Dungeon Monitors* who could be called on if things went a little too far or anyone got out of line. A bar sat along one wall boasting a sign that said, *"Three drink maximum"* and tables were placed around various stages throughout the room. In the back of the room sat a main stage with what seemed to be several tables. There were even chains hanging from the ceilings. Just then, an older man pulled a younger woman on a leash onto the stage and hooked her wrist straps to the chains above. He stepped behind her with what looked like a paddle, lifted her skirt and began spanking her. Several onlookers watched with enthusiasm, their own slaves sitting on the floor next to them.

I was really hoping Mike didn't like this because I was starting to feel a bit queasy and out of place. Scared even. I hadn't noticed I'd stopped moving until I felt a gentle tug on my arm. It was Mike urging me to follow. I hurried up next to him and shot him an irritated glare. He swatted my behind playfully.

We sat at an empty table between the main stage on our right, and a smaller stage to the left. The stage on the left was more hidden from the entrance. There, a man was tied to a table and two women were pouring hot wax on his chest. I held back a shocked gasp.

Mike looked around before offering me a chair. Alyssa did the same with Gabe. Not all the Doms made their charges sit on the cold, dirty cement floor, only the more sadistic ones evidently.

Alyssa seemed to be enjoying the role playing when the practically nude sub waitress showed up. Clearly under charge of the bald, six-foot-something, built-like-a-tank bartender who had a series of whips hanging on the wall behind his bar.

"Get my Gabe a beer in a doggy bowl, and I'll have a Sea Breeze," Alyssa said easily, fully immersing herself into the role of Gabe's Mistress.

The waitress' attention turned to Mike obediently.

Mike was trying not to burst out laughing at Alyssa's request. "I'll have a screwdriver and she'll have a tequila sunrise."

My eyes grew big. Mike knew I couldn't handle my liquor. One tequila sunrise would undoubtedly ensure I would be unconscious before nine. After the waitress left he leaned over to me. "You'll sip when I say."

I found myself both shocked and excited by his order. Then I knew why he said it. An older male, in his late forties, early- fifties, had sat down next to us with a younger man in tow. The younger man looked at the floor obediently, yet seemed very alert for any order he might be given.

I looked down, too, letting Mike and Alyssa do their thing.

The man's gaze was on me. He was looking me up and down. "What a beautiful *specimen* you have here. I sincerely hope you're going to scene with her tonight."

I felt the burning in my cheeks and my heart skipped a beat.

Mike shrugged casually. "I haven't decided yet."

The man leaned over to his slave and began massaging his swollen manhood. I turned my head in embarrassment. I noticed Mike and Gabe did, too. Alyssa, cool as a cucumber, just smiled and watched.

"You have a fine *specimen* there yourself," she said. "Do you bring your *playthings* here often?"

The man nodded. "I usually bring one of my girls, but male submissives are such a treat and seem to be rarer at *Kat 09*. Will you be putting your boy on display tonight Mistress…"

Alyssa reached her hand over the table, "Mistress Alyssa. And this is Master Mike."

He took Alyssa's hand delicately and shook it and gave a curt nod to Mike, who didn't offer his hand. "I'm Master Reginald Mathers."

"Your name is familiar to me," Mike said.

"As a Dom you've probably read some of my books about training subs."

My eyes popped open. *Someone writes books about this stuff?*

"Ah," Mike said with a flourish and a smile. His eyes caught mine for a brief second. It was clearly lust I saw there, wasn't it? Men.

Alyssa just sat back and observed, I noticed. Our drinks came. I busied myself watching, amused, as Gabriel tried to drink his beer from a bowl not using his hands (as per Alyssa's orders), occasionally giving Alyssa a sideways glare. She merely kept smiling and listening in on the discussion between Mike and Master Reg. Reg was explaining how to make a submissive more responsive to the paddle. Evidently paddles were his thing.

I seriously didn't understand the need for clubs like this, let alone public displays. For me, sex had always been something special between two people, no matter how kinky (or in my case, not). It was something to explore behind closed doors. I made sure not to pay attention to any of the stages. It was just too creepy. If any of this excited me at all, it was about Mike. He was the one who excited me. Not whips, crops or paddles or being submissive, but rather the idea that *he* was the one wielding the crop or giving me orders. There was something tantalizing about him taking charge of me. It seemed to wake some primal desire deep inside. Of course it would never work outside the bedroom, I quickly decided. No. I was far too independent for *that*.

"Well here, let me show you." Master Reg stood up and produced something from behind his back. I realized what it was when I suddenly found myself blindfolded.

I gasped in surprise, but felt Mike's hand on my arm patting me reassuringly. He whispered into my ear, "Red, remember your safe word and use it if you need to, babe."

I practically didn't comprehend what Mike was saying because my mind was still on the blindfold and Master Reg's boldness. There was something really wrong with a guy who carried a blindfold in his pocket. Just sayin'...

"Bring her up here," I heard Reg command.

"Why not?" Mike stood, lifting me with him. A cold rush of terror ran through me. Then I heard him whisper softly in my ear, "Trust me, I won't let it go too far. Safe word, remember?"

I took a deep breath, not sure whether to rip the blindfold off and smack Mike then and there, or wait. What the hell did he think he was doing? Yeah, we needed to talk to Reg because he knew where Eric was, and Eric was the key to either unloading or un-cursing the items currently sitting somewhere in the mountains just a few miles west of Genesee, but this had already gone beyond *too far*.

I felt Mike lead me up the stairs, carefully guiding me step-by-step. Then someone grabbed my arm and pulled me roughly into position, bringing the arm behind me.

Master Reg laughed. "You spoil this one," he said. It was clearly a comment aimed toward the padded, comfortable wrist cuffs I was wearing. He gently and firmly pulled my other arm behind my back. There was a clanking of chains and my arms were bound behind me, to the ceiling. The chain was pretty long and I could feel the slight pull. It was a good thing I did yoga, otherwise I imagined it might have been more uncomfortable, even painful.

I heard something scraping across the floor. My mind raced trying to figure out what it was. Next thing I knew, I was leaning over a small table or sawhorse of some sort. The back of my dress was lifted up. The crimson pooled in my cheeks. I really thought, in that moment, that I would die from embarrassment. Surely the entire audience was watching my cleavage, not to mention my bare ass in the air (pardon my candor).

"So you want to tease her with the paddle by gently rubbing..." Reg was saying.

I felt something soft on my rear. I didn't know whether to scream at Mike (maybe a stiletto to the shin?), be angry, or be excited. My body was responding in ways I hadn't anticipated or wanted. A tight smack from the leather paddle hit me square in the left cheek. Then the soft, gentle rubbing again. Another quick smack. I fought back the urge to cry out with each smack. I also felt myself getting turned on. He wasn't really smacking me *that* hard.

Mike seemed in no hurry to get me out of my predicament. "So do you find the paddle more enticing? I prefer a riding crop," he was saying. "She doesn't seem to mind it."

Just then I felt a searing sting across my right cheek. What the hell was he doing?

"If you start them off with the harsher whips you could risk injuring her or scaring her off of them. Be careful with canes, too. You have to train her body to respond."

Mike was *so* in trouble the second we walked out of here.

"I see what you're saying," Mike said as he lightly feathered the crop over the delicate skin high up between my thighs.

I could feel the goose bumps rising and my nipples harden.

"This one seems relatively well turned out. Very obedient and quiet," Reg said.

"I have to admit, she's the very first one I've trained," said Mike. "She's very obedient because she knows my punishments can be severe."

"Not bad for a first timer."

Mike rubbed my rear, moving his hand between my legs and beneath my panties and into a very private spot. Right in front of Master Reg. Now I was even more embarrassed, not only because some stranger had seen my boyfriend touch my private bits, but because both Mike and Reg knew just how turned on I really was. "Say, do you know Eric Baca?"

"I do as a matter of fact," Reg replied.

Mike moved his hand to my hip. "I knew that's where I'd heard your name before. Eric and I use to work together at the highway department. I know his old lady, Margie, too. I haven't seen either of them in a while since I moved down to Littleton."

"You heard they called it quits?"

"Oh really? That's unfortunate. They seemed a good couple. Anyway, Eric was a good guy to work with. I'd love to catch up with him sometime." Then I felt the paddle square on both cheeks this time. The surprise of it caused me to yelp.

"I might have one of his cards. But in the meantime I'm going to go talk to that beautiful Domme you have with you. I wonder if she'd turn submissive for me."

Mike laughed. "Good luck with that."

"You two have fun and when you're done, come back and join us." I heard Reg's heavy boots move off the stage.

The paddle stung me again. Each swat followed by his gentle touch. "Just relax, babe. We have to put on a little show so we aren't thrown out on our asses."

For what seemed like a half hour, Mike had his fun and I tried to lose myself, pretending he and I were alone. I was able to enjoy myself a little more then. Finally, he released me, helping me down the stairs, still blindfolded. I was still reeling from the experience and not sure if I wanted to send Mike home or drag him straight to bed when we got back to his place. When we got back to the table, Mike helped me sit down. He leaned over to my ear. "Sorry, I'll make it up to you later, but we had to look convincing or this guy would have been suspicious. Now tell me, Yes Master, I'll be a good girl."

A wave of relief washed over me. Quite uncomfortably I complied and said, "Yes, Master. I'll be a good girl."

He petted my hair and removed the blindfold, handing it back to Reg, who looked pleased with my performance. My bottom was sore and the chair was no longer comfortable. Gabe looked positively mortified and seemed to be trying to make himself seem as small as possible. Especially since Alyssa was now stroking the paddle Mike had brought back down from the stage.

Alyssa smiled brightly at Mike. "Did you know that Reg knows Eric?"

Mike nodded, taking a sip of his drink. I looked at the tequila sunrise in front of me. "You may have three sips," he told me.

I took exactly three sips and followed Gabe's example.

"So were you in Eric and Margie's group?" Mike asked Reg.

Alyssa kind of choked on her drink. "They didn't have a group Mike. It was just them." She smiled at Reg. "We practice something similar."

"As do I," he said, taking a drink. "Yes. Have you tried any of Eric's enchanted training equipment?"

The question took us all by surprise. Mike shook his head. "Eric never shared with me that he and Margie were into the scene. But then I wasn't either until recently, thanks to Alyssa."

Alyssa smiled. "You're welcome."

Reg laughed at Alyssa's quick wit. "He makes delightfully enchanted whips and devices to make more obedient submissives. You should get back in touch with him. He's living here in Denver now."

Finally! I breathed a very inward sigh of relief. This was the information we wanted.

Reg pulled two cards out of his wallet and handed them to Mike. "The first is Eric's new contact information. The second is my information. If you ever need some training tips you can bring this pretty little thing to my dungeon for some private lessons."

Like hell, I thought.

Alyssa beamed at Reg.

Reg turned his full attention to her. "Now you, Mistress. Any chance I can talk you into my dungeon for a role reversal? On your part I mean."

Alyssa laughed. "Not likely. I'm unbreakable."

He shook his head. "I've had quite a few Domme's *switch* in my dungeon, sweetheart. You think about it." With that, he pushed another one of his cards across the table at her. Then he stood and looked at Mike. "Look Eric up, just be sure that if you buy anything from him, don't piss him off."

Then wordlessly Reg sauntered off toward the other side of the room, his sub following a few steps behind.

We finished our drinks (well, I took three more sips) and we left. I waited until we got into the car and Alyssa had pulled safely away before I punched Mike in the shoulder. "That's for allowing that freak to chain me up and smack my ass!"

I smacked him on the cheek then (not hard, I hit like a girl). "That is for…" I paused noticing Alyssa and

Gabe were really quiet in the front seat. "You know what that's for!"

Mike didn't argue. "I deserved that. I'm sorry. I didn't think it was that much of a big deal."

"Not a big deal? How about I bare your ass in public and give you a spanking with paddles and whips? Maybe expose your naughty bits to some stranger. Huh?" I put my hands over my chest, glaring at Alyssa when I realized she was watching me in the rearview. She looked away quickly and started laughing uncontrollably.

"That's not funny, Liss. That guy got a full view of my vajayjay because Mike here, was getting hot and decided to give me a little rub down."

Her laughing slowly subsided. "I think it was the use of the phrase *naughty bits* that got me going. I'm sorry," she said then started howling with laughter again.

Mike put his hand on my knee. "I'm sorry. That's all I can say. We got what we went for."

Maybe *he* did. Even so, I couldn't deny that I was still a bit turned on by the whole evening. I looked out the window and didn't speak the rest of the way home. Alyssa and Gabe tried to lighten the mood by talking about new restaurants and clubs in the area.

When Alyssa and Gabe dropped us off in Mike's driveway I was still pissed. Now out of the stilettos, I carried them in one hand and stomped up the front walk in just stockings, shoving my key into the door. I heard Mike talking to Alyssa, and heard her pulling out of the driveway. Mike came up behind me.

I got into the house and threw my shoes on the floor then stomped to the kitchen for a glass of water.

"Look, I know you're pissed but you knew it was a possibility before we went in," he reasoned.

"Seriously, Mike? You were enjoying yourself!" I accused. That's when I realized that more than being bared and spanked in public, it was that he seemed to enjoy it that upset me. Or perhaps I was just pretending to be upset because good girls didn't go to BDSM clubs and enjoy it when their boyfriend worked them over with a paddle in front of strangers.

"You're right. I was enjoying it. But so were you," he said simply and retreated to the bedroom.

I had nothing to say to that. I couldn't argue with him. I really had enjoyed allowing Mike dominate me. It was a side of myself I'd never explored or experienced. Nor expected.

Resigned, I followed him into the bedroom. "Fine, I did enjoy it, but only because it was you."

A slow smile spread on his lips. "Likewise."

"But I think at this point we need to make a pact."

Mike stopped undoing his pants and looked at me.

"No more BDSM clubs. At home in the bedroom, fine. *Never again* in public."

He smiled. "Fine, I agree. But since we're home and you're all dressed up, go get those heels back on and get back in here." He gave me a coy smile.

A rush of excitement ran through me. "Fine." I did as I was told and that night Mike explored his dominant side and I my submissive side and neither of us got to bed until after two that morning.

CHAPTER NINE
SUNDAY, JULY 2

The next morning I awoke wrapped in Mike's arms. It was Saturday. I yawned, noticing a large brown spider crawling on the wall. I got up, grabbed a flyswatter from under the bed where I stashed it, and crawled out of bed naked to kill it. Not a second after the spider fell dead onto the carpet I heard Mike chuckling.

"Damn spiders," I said. "You need an exterminator."

"I need to spray the perimeter of the house with spider spray. I'll pick some up this weekend and do it. Hey, come back here."

I grabbed a tissue and picked up the spider carcass, running it into the bathroom to flush down the toilet.

"You look incredibly cute killing spiders naked," he called after me.

"You're a comedian."

"Someone needs her coffee. I'll get up and make it. You have a shower." He leaned into the bathroom as I flushed the toilet, making sure the spider was going down. He kissed my cheek, then my lips before leaving the bathroom for the kitchen, completely nude.

"Mmmm." I set the flyswatter with spider guts on the edge of the bathroom sink and turned around to look at my rear in the mirror. It was still a little pink. "I think you bruised my bum."

"Sorry, babe. Didn't mean to," he called from the kitchen. I thought I heard him chuckle.

With a sigh, I jumped into the shower and got myself cleaned up. We had a plan to make today. A plan that involved talking to Eric and somehow getting him to either take the stuff back or un-curse the amulets and spirit board hidden somewhere up in the mountains on a remote piece of private property.

●

Mike called Eric Baca. Clearly if the guy was deep into that scene, he would much prefer talking to another Dom. Or at least that was our thinking. I sat at the dining room table with a cup of coffee listening to Mike's end of the conversation.

"Mr. Baca? Yeah, my name is Mike Katz. Reginald Mathers gave me your card. He said you had some impressive bdsm equipment for sale. Enchanted. I'm interested."

I watched Mike's face contort into slight annoyance, then resignation.

"That's fine. I can be there then, and I'll bring my sub."

I gave him my classic what-the-fuck and he shrugged helplessly. "Ah, okay. Thank you, see you then."

Mike clicked off the phone.

"Oh no! What do you mean you'll bring your sub? Remember we had a deal..." I stood up with a warning glare and considered, briefly, dousing him with my cup of coffee.

"Relax! The guy only sells to couples by appointment only because a lot of his equipment needs to be fit to the person it's meant for. He put emphasis on the *fit.*" Mike looked apologetic. "Don't worry, you'll be fully clothed in normal street clothes and I'll make sure the guy knows we're not into the lifestyle twenty-four-seven, right? We just have to go and talk to him."

I sighed. My irritation vanished and I sat back down. "So we get there, he shows us his enchanted collection and then what? We say, *Oh, by the way, we have some of your enchanted items and we're pretty sure they're cursed. Can you take the curse off, please? I'd like to wear that beautiful amulet your ex-girlfriend gave me.*"

Mike laughed. "Well, when you put it that way it sounds far-fetched. Maybe even a little ridiculous." He held up a finger, "But, leave it to me. I'll find some way to at least find out how he enchanted it. Didn't you say if you know how something was made you can likely unmake it?"

I nodded. "Yes, in theory. But who's to say he's going to share his secrets with some guy off the street?"

"I'm good at getting people to open up. I have interrogation training, remember?"

I giggled. "We can't water board him."

"Ha-ha! Very funny." He poured himself a fresh cup of coffee. "We're meeting him at four."

I pulled my hair back and shook my head.

"What? Oh ye of little faith." He laughed and went into the living room and plopped onto the couch, turning the television on.

●

The scent of oiled leather permeated Eric Baca's small shop. Well, really it wasn't so much a shop as it was a room attached to the garage of his rented one story house. It wasn't a comfortable room either. Have you ever been into one of those 'couple's' shops with all the sex toys? Yeah - it was something like that but in tighter quarters with whips, ball gags, and various restraint devices. Needless to say I was pretty uncomfortable. Even Mike seemed a bit taken aback.

"So what were you interested in?" Baca was saying.

Mike immediately looked toward some benign looking riding crops. "Perhaps some whips and some additional restraining devices, I think." He turned to me, "Babe?"

"Yeah," I agreed with a quick smile, thankful Mike had decided to not go with something more mortifying. Like a sex swing or one of the sex machines. I tried to keep my eyes on the floor.

"We met Mathers at Kat-O-Nine. He recommended you. It seems we practice a similar religion," Mike was saying in a candid tone.

Eric nodded. "Daemon worshipers or Satanists?"

"Daemons," Mike replied, as if it was a conversation he had every day. I smiled at his nonchalance.

"Then you might be interested in this collar of Asmodeus." Baca reached up and pulled down a very light and delicate leather choker decorated with a Tiger's Eye carved with the sigil of Asmodeus.

My hand automatically moved toward it. It called to me.

Baca handed it to me. "It suits you."

I put it up to my neck practically unbidden.

Mike nodded. "I like it. It's pretty and it almost glows…we'll take it."

Baca nodded in agreement. "Good. I do believe pieces choose their wearers."

My mind went to the amulets; the entire reason we were here. "Yeah, but you made the amulets for Margie, so is it the same way when you make someone for someone specific?"

I was painfully aware of both men's eyes on me. Mike's in sheer terror and Eric's in complete surprise. I figured changing the subject at this point was moot. The cat was out of the bag. Some undercover agent I was. "Yeah, um, Margie gave us some amulets and a few other things when she moved."

Eric shook his head. I was half expecting him to kick us out of his house. He didn't. Instead he sat down on a desk. "Well you be careful of anything she gave you. This is between us, you understand? Don't trust that woman as far as you could throw her. She has a nasty habit of throwing curses for the slightest infractions."

Mike and I exchanged glances and I handed him the choker collar. "To be honest, that's also a part of the reason we wanted to talk to you. We think some of the stuff she gave me was cursed, but when she told us you made it for her and that's why she was getting rid of it, we thought maybe you cursed it and you could take the curse off."

"Not to mention Reg Mathers told us to be careful of your training equipment if we pissed you off. Mentioned it was enchanted?" Mike added.

Eric nodded and looked around as if there might be someone around who could hear. He lowered his voice. "I see. Look," he stood up, "Bring *the stuff* over sometime later in the week and I'll take a look at it and see if I can help remove the curse on whatever it is, but so you know, I think the bitch cursed me, too. I know kind of how she works so maybe we can do a rite of unmaking, but I make no guarantees. We did a lot of experimentation with that sort of thing when we were together. As for everything I make," he pointed to the beautiful choker collar Mike held, "It all goes through a rite of making, but I only infuse the items with sexual energy, nothing more. I will magickally charge stuff for more specific purposes if people ask or if I'm making something for a friend. Or I won't charge them at all if someone tells me not to."

"That's good to know," I said, finding myself a bit more at ease standing amidst the floggers, single tail whips, paddles, spreader bars, chokers, cuffs and other paraphernalia. I was comfortable talking Daemons, rituals, and curses. It was only the sex talk that made my prudish side uncomfortable.

"So how much for the choker?" Mike asked.

"Forty-five. Anything else?"

Mike looked around. He pointed to the wall. "Flogger?"

"Good choice. Here," Baca took the flogger down and handed it to Mike.

Mike shifted it from hand to hand, feeling the weight (or something). "I like this one."

"Excellent. That's another sixty five." Eric Baca started writing up a receipt and Mike pulled out his wallet.

He paid cash and tucked the receipt into his pocket. "Here, just so you have my contact information," Mike handed him a card. "How about Thursday night?"

That was Mike, always handing out those damn cards. I fought the urge to shake my head.

Baca examined the card for a minute. "Wait, you're a cop? Is there something more going on here?"

"No, not at all. This really is a personal visit, we really are Daemonolaters I promise. It's just my cell number is on the card there, and I happen to be a detective," Mike assured him. He took down Eric Baca's number and then they agreed we should get together with the items on

Thursday night to see if Eric could unmake them. This, of course, meant we would have to contact Gabe and Alyssa to bring them back down from the mountains.

With that, we left and I'm pretty sure Eric Baca watched us until our car drove out of sight.

"So I love how people get all freaky on you when they find out you're in law enforcement. Do you get that a lot?" I asked. It just never occurred to me how difficult it could be to make friends without them acting all freaky. After all, I imagined not everyone was on the right side of the law.

Mike shrugged. "Usually. People only expect to see law enforcement when they've done something wrong or something bad happens. So I think it's a natural reaction to get nervous around authority figures."

"Well I don't get it. You don't make me nervous at all," I said with a pleased smile. I caught him looking at me out of the corner of his eye.

"That's true. You weren't even nervous around me when I came knocking at your door asking you about Daemonolatry and murder." He chuckled. "I suppose that's probably why we hit it off from the get-go."

"Did we?" I thought back to my first encounter with Mike. I didn't recall us hitting it off. As a matter-of-fact, I kind of thought our beginning was a bit rocky. After all, Mike kind of annoyed me at first and made me nervous as hell. But I didn't tell him that. Instead I gave him a less brutal truth. "I remember being freaked out to find you at my door. I also remember Mike the skeptic thinking I was nuts."

He laughed. "I never thought you were nuts. Maybe just a little creative."

CHAPTER TEN
MONDAY, JULY 3

I was just as surprised as Mike was to find Gary Smith standing at the door Monday morning and he wasn't smiling.

"Gary, we weren't expecting you. What are you doing here?" Mike opened the door wide and motioned him to enter.

"I wish this was a social visit Mike, but it's not. We have a problem." Gary gave a nervous glance in my direction.

Something bad was about to go down – I could feel it.

"You know a guy named Eric Baca?"

Mike nodded. "Yeah. Long story, but yeah."

"Well it better be one hell of a story buddy, because he was found murdered last night with a bullet suggesting it was a police issued handgun, and it seems you were either the last person to see him alive or he was trying to call you."

"Son-of-a-bitch." Mike stared at Gary in disbelief.

"Man, I know. It's crazy, but I told my captain I'd bring you and Liz down to the station and we'd get it all sorted out. I know there has to be a logical explanation."

Gary patted Mike on the shoulder. "I'll wait while you to grab whatever you might need.

"Liz has to come, too?"

"If she's your alibi, yeah. Probably a good idea."

Mike nodded. "Okay."

We went willingly to the police station and complied when we were separated into different rooms. I felt a spark of hope when Detective Smith, a good friend of Mike's and now a friend of mine, came into the room. "Hey Liz."

"Hey Gary." I gave his a forced smile.

"How long have you known Eric Baca?" he started. Once again I was stuck in the middle of a murder investigation.

I shrugged. "Just met him. Mike and I went to his shop to talk to him about his ex-girlfriend and some items she gave me. We're trying to find her to give some of it back."

"And you thought he would know where she was?"

Duh, yeah, that's what I was getting at. But I didn't say that. "Well, they travel in the same circles."

"The bdsm folks," Gary finished for me with a raised eyebrow.

I felt my cheeks flush several shades of crimson. "Um, yeah."

"People who we talked to from the club said you and Mike looked like old pros..."

I cut him off, mortified he was putting me and Mike's sex life under a microscope. "Gary, I assure you it may have appeared real to outsiders, but it was supposed to. Evidently we're better actors than we thought. It was all about finding Eric Baca to find his ex-girlfriend and maybe get more information on the stuff she gave me."

"What stuff?"

"Some..." I lingered for a moment. "Ritual supplies."

"What is so important about the ritual supplies she gave you?"

I couldn't mask the exasperated sigh. Here I was, being put in a position to explain my beliefs again. "She's a Daemonolater and she gave me some items from her ex, Eric, that were cursed. We were trying to find him or her so we could either break the curse or give the stuff back to him or her." It sounded ridiculous when I said it aloud. I knew how Gary Smith felt about my religion. He usually just pretended Mike and I weren't into the occult at all. I began to seriously question at that moment if Gary just tolerated me because of Mike, but secretly disapproved of our relationship.

"Cursed?" he asked. His face didn't even flinch.

I nodded. I was afraid to say anything else. Things are a lot different when you're on the other side of the table.

"Can't you just stop believing in a curse and break it? Or isn't there some kind of spell you can use to banish it or something?"

I swallowed, hard. "Yeah, we tried all that."

"Why not just throw the items away? Why the elaborate charade as a bdsm couple and the visit to a bdsm shop where you actually purchased," he looked down at his notepad, "A flogger and a collar?"

I seriously thought I was going to die from embarrassment. I decided to start with the first question and try to skirt the last. "Destroying them wouldn't work, we tried, and throwing them away left open the potential that someone else would find them and take on cursed items unknowingly. I have a conscience."

Gary nodded. "And the purchase of the flogger and collar?"

I wasn't getting out of it that easily. "Mike and I needed to seem legitimate and didn't want to look like we were fishing for information. Besides, the collar was pretty," I told him, proud of my own newfound bravado.

"Wouldn't he have known you were fishing when you mentioned the items?"

He was right, I couldn't deny that. "It's really complicated."

Gary sat down and leaned across the table toward me. "Liz, you and Mike are my friends. I really want to help Mike and you, but you first have to start by telling me everything. I don't think you realize how serious this is. You guys are suspects in a murder investigation."

"You think Mike and I did this?" The disbelief felt like plaster on my face.

"You have to realize how it looks," Gary started.

I cut him off, again. "You don't honestly believe that we killed that man?"

Gary shook his head. "No, of course not, but it's not me you have to convince. It's the DA and the other detectives who think you two are looking awfully guilty right now."

It was at that point I took a deep breath and told Gary everything. From the initial call from Margie to picking up the items, to discovering they were cursed, to our search for Eric at the club, then the subsequent visit to Eric's shop. "We didn't even know Eric Baca was dead until you showed up on our doorstep," I finished. My entire body felt numb.

"Is that everything?" Gary asked.

I nodded.

"Since we have no tangible evidence to hold you on, I suggest you stick around in town and make yourself available to us if we have any more questions," he told me.

"Can I go?"

Gary nodded, stood, and led me out to the lobby where Mike was pacing, waiting for me. He looked me over as if to make sure I was okay, then he pulled Gary aside and they talked for about fifteen minutes. Then Gary drove us home. The drive home was dead silent, both of us completely lost in thought and Gary not daring to say a word.

I was still in shock when we finally arrived at the house. I wandered inside and sat down in the living room.

Mike stayed behind and talked to Gary on the porch, running into the bedroom and back out again. After about fifteen minutes he came in and sat down beside me on the couch. "I talked to Smith and he agrees."

I didn't say anything.

"We need to meet with Reg Mathers again, undercover. Find out who really did this," he said. Then he clarified as if he needed to, "You and me, I mean."

I felt my head slowly turn toward him. His eyes widened. I imagine I must have looked like I was just coming off the set of *The Exorcist*. I felt my face contort into an incredibly bitchy scowl and my voice changed, almost sounding Daemonic. "Seriously? The guy who wanted to introduce me to his *dungeon*?"

Then Mike gave me *that* look. The look that made me resign and give in to anything he wanted because I knew, ultimately, he knew the ins and outs of detective work and going undercover better than I did. "Liz, come on. I know you said no more clubs. I know you don't want to play in public. I know we agreed only in the bedroom, but our very lives are at stake. Worst case scenario we could end up in prison over this. In the very least I could lose my job and your boss might have second thoughts about you, too, by the time the detectives are done sifting through every aspect of your life." He looked at me with pleading eyes.

I sighed, resigned to the fact that he was right. We were murder suspects and the only way to prove we were innocent was to go in and find out who really killed Eric. I was beginning to hate and resent those damn cursed objects even more. "Fine," I finally mumbled.

I looked over at him. Mike knew more than I did. That was clear by the way he was biting his lip; a habitual tick he seemed to develop whenever he was working on a difficult case.

"How did we become suspects anyway?" I was actually shaking. "Because we were there yesterday?"

"We were the last ones to see him alive and they placed his time of death around the same time we were there. He was shot with a police issued hand gun." Mike's face was blank. He stared off into the black hole of the fireplace.

"Yours?" A rush of fear ran through me.

He shook his head. "No. All my guns are accounted for and I handed both my guns over to Gary, but they won't match the fired shell casings they recovered on scene."

I'd seen enough *Law & Order* to know we were suspects based on circumstantial evidence only. It was likely we'd be ruled out by something...wasn't it? I was too afraid to ask.

Mike seemed to pick up on this. "Don't worry, babe. There's no way they can pin this on us. We just need to make sure our defense is air tight so we don't get screwed on a technicality."

But he didn't sound as sure as I wanted him to sound. I got up and called my boss. I was going to need to take my entire month of vacation time. Between losing my house to the tornado and now this, there was no way around it.

CHAPTER ELEVEN
TUESDAY, JULY 4

You'd think a bdsm club wouldn't be open on the fourth of July and you'd be wrong. I didn't want to have to go back to the club. I didn't. But that was the only place Reg Mathers would agree to meet us. Evidently they were having an Independence Day celebration all week long at *Kat 09*. He'd given Mike the excuse that he was giving demonstrations at the club all week and didn't have the time to meet anywhere else. It sounded like a load of crap to me. With Alyssa's help I managed to pull together something more conservative, yet sexy that was still safe as club-wear. It was a mid-thigh black skirt with matching panties, that damn pair of stilettos (again), and thigh high stockings with a garter belt. It was still too revealing for my usual level of modesty. At least it said, according to Alyssa, that I was there for a drink, not play.

Mike and I found parking on the street almost immediately and wandered into the club around eight that night. No one really seemed to pay attention when we walked into the dank depths and found ourselves a table near the bar. We ordered a pitcher of beer. If that didn't say 'no play' I wasn't sure what did. When Mike spotted Reg he gave him a polite nod. Reg immediately excused himself from the table he was at and came over to ours. Meanwhile, the waitress brought us a pitcher of beer and three glasses.

Reg looked around suspiciously as if someone would overhear. "I can't believe Eric is dead. I liked him. He was a nice guy I can't believe the police thought you two had something to do with it."

"Well, evidently we were the last ones to see him alive. We stopped by his workshop for some supplies. Evidently he was shot and a similar gun is registered to me. Do you know anyone who would hate him that much?" Mike didn't elaborate or admit he was a cop even though by the way Reg was acting it seemed like he may have known already.

There was an uncomfortable span of silence. At least Mike got straight to the point. I had a feeling I should add something to the conversation, but kept my mouth firmly shut. I was in way over my head and felt it was better to let Mike handle this. It was, after all, his day job to solve crimes.

"Cops asked me the same thing. I honestly can't think of anyone. Could it have been Margie?" Reg asked helpfully. It was almost too helpful for my taste.

I got a bad feeling in my gut. Probably meaning Margie had something to do with it. My abilities weren't always so forthcoming, but today they seemed right on cue.

"Why do you say that?" Mike bit his lip. I could see Mike's mind racing with that possibility.

Reg shrugged. "You've met Marge. She's a real bitch when she's been crossed. Rumor has it Eric was cheating on her, so she thought. He claims she was cheating on him. I suspect it's probably very true. That's why they broke up to begin with. No trust."

"There's a difference between being a bitch to an unfaithful mate as opposed to killing them," I said absently, then realized both men were looking at me. "Sorry," I said quickly.

"No, I don't mean a bitch as in bitchy like starting rumors or crying about the break up. I mean she is notorious for cursing people," Reg explained. He lifted a beer filled glass to his lips and took a drink. "She's good at it."

I saw Mike's eyebrow lift in question. That was Mike - always the skeptic. Despite our current situation he was still willing to roll his eyes at someone else's mention of a curse. Of course his experiences were real, it was now only everyone else who was suspect. "How do you know she's good at it?"

"About seven months ago she and one of the female members of a Cthulhu cult got into it and next thing we know," he paused long enough to make the slit-throat gesture, "the other girl ended up getting into a car accident and dying. That's for starters."

Mike was smiling now, clearly in disbelief. "Well, that could have been a coincidence."

Reg nodded. "I suppose. It still doesn't explain why one of my friends fell deathly ill with a rare strain of pneumonia after having a tiff with her. Or why her own mother ended up dead only two weeks after her father died and after she and Margie had a dispute over the inheritance."

"How well do you know Margie?" Mike leaned in toward Reg, grabbing his own glass of beer.

"Not well at all. But I know a lot of people around her and she has a reputation." Reg shook his head. "I wouldn't mess with her. She purports to be a sub, but she tops from the bottom, and she's vindictive. She outed one of the members of Temple Asmodai to the partners in his firm. Was a successful lawyer before that. Might still be, I don't know. But the point is they asked for his resignation because they didn't want the information getting out into the media."

My ears perked up. I'd heard rumors of the infamous Asmodai sect. Even heard some of their members were OTS, but I'd never been privy to the inner workings of the group let alone who counted themselves among the membership. I had my suspicions of course. Several years ago during the meeting with some members of another order I was asked, by a man my father's age, if I practiced sex magick. I suspected he was probably a member. Obviously sex magick wasn't my forte and the Asmodai group was just that - a sex magick cult. I'd also heard whisperings of inner orders and offshoot orders. No doubt about it, sex magick was big, but it wasn't always openly talked about. Not that most occultists were loose lipped anyway. After all, the whole of regular mainstream society was still pretty much oblivious to how many of us there actually were, or if they were aware, simply didn't care one way or the other.

"Does she blackmail people often? Maybe someone could be framing her?" Mike suggested. He started biting his lip. I could see the gears in his brain turning and his eyes almost looked through Reg.

It was actually a pretty good theory. Or at least I thought so.

Reg shrugged, kind of fidgeting in Mike's gaze. "It's possible. I've only heard of her doing that to that one guy."

Mike produced a pad of paper and a pen from his back pocket. "What's the guy's name and do you know how I can get ahold of him?"

"His name is Jack Barringer." Reg shrugged. "He worked for Schlesinger and Monroe. I'm betting they're in the book. They might be able to help with that. Otherwise, I don't have his contact info."

I pulled out my phone and did a quick Internet search. Schlesinger and Monroe, Attorneys at Law, was the second one down. I enlarged the page and pointed it in Mike's direction. He took down the phone number. If it came right down to it, I could always call my lawyer friend Mark, who was also a Daemonolater. Speaking of Mark, I hadn't really talked to him in over a month after I called to make sure he and his wife's house had been repaired after the fire three months ago. I made a mental note to call him at some point. He didn't even know my own house had been demolished by the freak tornado.

"Anything else you think might be helpful?" Mike asked. He was starting to sound more cop-like the further we got into the conversation.

This wasn't lost on Reg, who seemed to be getting antsy. "Or you can talk to Minerva Layton. She knows him." He gave Mike the number.

I sat quietly and checked my e-mail. How I lived without a smart phone before smart phones was beyond me. I liked feeling plugging in and connected to everyone. I was never alone and never bored.

Mike took down this new information and nodded. "So can I call you if I have any more questions? Liz and I have agreed to the no-club thing so this is uncomfortable for her."

Reg chuckled. "That's too bad. I take it her first experience was..." he paused before saying, "Unpleasant?"

Mike glanced at me. "Something like that."

"That's fine then, call me anytime." He nodded toward me. "You spoil that one. Part of the point of submitting is giving up control to someone you trust who will test your comfort zone," he said to me.

I didn't know what to say. Was he actually trying to have some sort of philosophical bdsm conversation with me? I looked down at the table instead.

"You have to trust in Master Mike to know what is best for you, to know what you need, and to provide you with what you need. When he takes you out of your comfort zone or tests your limitations and boundaries, you need to trust that he will always keep you safe and out of harm's way. That's also why submission isn't always easy. Trust isn't easy," Reg continued.

How little Reg knew. He had no idea just how much trust I was putting into Mike right now in hopes that Mike could get himself out from underneath a possible homicide charge and get me out of the accomplice category. Sure, their evidence was circumstantial at best and we could probably prove reasonable doubt, but Mike wasn't taking any chances. He'd seen people convicted on circumstantial evidence and he'd mentioned that a jury might not be too sympathetic to two people allegedly into bdsm. I paused and corrected my thoughts, two people who *are* into bdsm. Evidently that was almost as taboo to the average conservative redneck as being homosexual. I had no doubt he was doing what was best for both of us. Finding the real killer was the best way to remove all doubt. I managed to give Reg a weak smile. "I'll keep that in mind, thank you Sir."

Mike gave me a very subtle approving look. "I'll keep that in mind, too. Thank you."

"Oh, and another thing, if you're looking for Margie, you want to try *Abyss*. It's up past Central City." Reg gave Mike the address. "Private club. Talk to Damien, tell him I sent you. A lot of people there might be helpful with regard to Margie. It would also be a good place to test this little one's limits."

Mike nodded. "I'll do that. Thank you."

"Anytime." Reg winked at me.

I fought the urge to speak my mind and roll my eyes. Instead, I looked down at my hands and bit my tongue.

That's when Mike stood, thanked Reg for his time, and we left. Once we were outside in the fresh air I felt like I was able to breathe again.

"Anything about that seem strange to you?" He asked me once we were in the car.

"That whole place seems strange to me," I said, buckling myself in. I kicked off the stilettos. Finally, I said what needed to be said. "Do we really have to go to this private club?"

"I want to investigate first. Talk to Jack Barringer and Minerva Layton, then we'll decide if we need to go to Abyss. This all seems to be leading to Margie. In which case we need to find her and the private club might be the road to that." He checked his mirrors and pulled out into traffic, heading home. "I just want to know why we were framed for this."

That was the elephant in the room, or rather the car, wasn't it? Someone had framed us and it had to be intentional. Someone who knew Mike was a detective.

I felt a little dizzy and tired and next thing I knew, there I stood in the red-black smoke in a dark space. I saw the Daemon, cloven hoofed and horned standing in the shadows. "You were convenient!" the male voice boomed.

I was still trying to get over the cliché appearance of the Daemon. I looked into the red, swirling depths of his eyes. "Convenient?" I parroted back.

Asmodeus lifted a sculpted eyebrow, stereotypically angular and sharp in appearance. "Quit being a simpleton, Elizabeth. You know better."

I wanted to pout and stomp my foot. It wasn't fair. It also wasn't fair that Daemons know what you're thinking without you having to say a word. Behaving like a spoiled brat in front of a Daemon did nothing but cause them to metaphorically 'roll their eyes'.

The Daemon crossed his arms over his chest and said, "Think about it. Why would Margie curse you? Why not give the items directly back to Eric? She gave them to you knowingly."

"She planned to kill him and needed a patsy to pin it on!" A cold chill ran up my arms.

The Daemon nodded, winked and gave me a toothy grin.

Then I felt myself fall backward into darkness. The wind was knocked out of me. I gasped for air. The light approached quickly, pulling me back into the car. I was sitting in the passenger seat in a cold sweat. Mike had pulled over to the side of the road.

"Liz," he yelled. His eyes were filled with concern and he was frowning.

I took several measured breaths and ran my hands through my hair.

"You scared the shit out of me! Don't do that while I'm driving." He sat back and handed me a half full bottled water from the center console. "What was it? A panic attack?"

"That wasn't a panic attack," I said in a frosty tone. "I didn't have a choice I was pulled into it."

"Another trance?"

"I prefer ascension. Unbidden ascension. Asmodeus had something to say." I looked straight ahead and took a drink from the water bottle. It was hot and tasted nasty. I almost spit it out.

"Anything useful?" Mike's tone suggested he'd just gone into disbelief mode. Any other time I might have found it endearing. Even refreshing. Today it just pissed me off.

"Margie framed us on purpose." I didn't offer anything else save for a deep sigh. Mike was starting to get on my nerves. That probably wasn't a good sign since before all this happened we'd been discussing the possibility of moving in together at some point in the future. However, I was pretty sure it wasn't going to work. How could I live with a man who, after a mere few days of living together, drove me nuts? And not in a good way.

Mike didn't say anything at first either. He pulled back into traffic and we drove about a block before he finally said, "That doesn't make sense."

"Yeah, you're right. It doesn't make sense." I agreed just because I didn't want to discuss it. Childish, perhaps, but it was probably the best thing I did that night – for both of us. Luckily most men seem to have a built in bitch-alarm. They know when they've gone too far and pissed you off because that's when they shut up and start being nice just to appease you. When we finally got home I decided not to stay up to watch fireworks. Neither of us was in the mood for anything festive. Instead, I went straight to bed and Mike left me alone.

CHAPTER TWELVE
WEDNESDAY, JULY 5

I've said it before and I'll say it again, things always look a lot brighter and more manageable after a good night's sleep. I know that I felt one hundred percent better when I woke up the next morning. Mike was still feeling overly cautious. I could tell because not only was the coffee made, but after I got my cup of coffee and sat down, a fresh plate of eggs and sausage was set in front of me.

"How are you feeling this morning?" He asked.

"Better," I admitted. I smiled at my own stupidity. I must have been pre-menstrual or something because at that moment I couldn't imagine myself living anywhere else except with Mike. Don't ask – it's a female thing. Hormones make us think, do and say crazy stuff sometimes. Never underestimate the power of the body's natural chemicals.

He handed me a fork and a paper napkin. "So are you in the mood to go run around today?"

I nodded and dug into my breakfast, surprised at how starved I felt. I paused from eating to ask to obvious question. "Yeah, what do you have planned?" It's not like I had anything else to do. After the accident and then losing the house, my boss told me to take all the time I needed. I still had vacation time saved up anyway.

"I hope you don't mind, but I called your buddy Mark this morning on the off chance he knew Jack Barringer and turns out they're golfing buddies. The guy went into private practice after he got fired. So thanks to Mark we have a lunch meeting with Mr. Barringer at noon, and we have a meeting with Ms. Minerva Layton at three-thirty. That's when she's finally done teaching classes for the day."

"Classes?"

"Evidently she teaches Junior High. She's teaching summer school." Mike shrugged, grabbing his own plate of eggs and sausage. He sat down next to me and began eating.

I shook my head. I wondered what a woman like that had to fear from the likes of Margie. Then it occurred to me the woman was a teacher who practiced sex magick in tandem with the occult. It was a no-brainer.

"What are you thinking?" Mike asked, giving me his signature perplexed look.

"Just everything." I let out a big sigh and went back to eating my breakfast.

"I'm sorry if I upset you last night."

"This whole thing has me upset," I said with a sigh. "It's not you. I'm just on edge and moody."

He nodded. "Would it make you feel better if I told you how much I loved you?" He smiled at me and I melted.

I leaned over and kissed him. "I love you, too."

"So how about a jog after breakfast and then we'll get ready for lunch?"

I choked on some egg. I hadn't been jogging since, well, I never jogged. "Can we walk? I don't jog."

He laughed. "Sure, we can walk. We'll just walk fast. Exercise releases endorphins and helps with stress relief."

With some reluctance I agreed and after breakfast we took a brisk walk along a greenbelt trail.

•

Jack Barringer was tall, lanky, and had a full head of blond hair. To be honest, he looked no older than twenty-five even though I knew he had to be in his thirties. He wore a black pair of slacks, dress shoes, and a blue silk tie with a white shirt. I don't know what it is but I don't trust anyone in a suit. Perhaps it was the fact that Jack looked like a Mormon missionary. Or maybe it was that he was a lawyer. Either way he had that vibe about him that made me want to wash my hands after shaking his.

Again, I sat there and let Mike take complete control of asking questions. I'd jump in if I needed to.

"So did Mark tell you what we wanted to meet with you about?" Mike asked, getting straight to the point.

Jack didn't seem to mind the fact that Mike was direct. "Yeah, Margie. That woman is nothing but trouble. Stay away from her."

"That's kind of vague. Could you be more specific?" Mike leaned in toward him.

The waitress showed up at the table and we ordered some sesame chicken, Mongolian beef, and moo shu pork along with fried rice.

Finally, once the waitress was gone and we had our drinks, Jack looked around, leaned into us and began telling the story. "Margie and I had a difference in opinion about something we were doing in a private group ritual. I ended up getting a lot of the group members on my side because what she wanted to do seemed unnecessarily kinky for an act of sex magick and we didn't see how it would further our intentions or enhance the magickal energy. So we dissented. She knew I was the ringleader and told me to watch my back. I guess you could say she blackmailed me. Either I let up and quit causing problems with her hand in the group rituals, or she was going to tell my bosses what I did. She'd even secretly taken some video and threatened to e-mail it to them. Of course the video was too dark to really see anything or identify participants."

He stopped and took a long drink of the iced tea in front of him. Setting the glass down, he took a deep breath and continued. "I wasn't going to give her the satisfaction, so I resigned from my job. I was starting my own practice anyway, though the rumors were that Margie had told my bosses and I was fired. I think she started those rumors herself just to scare her followers into submission. Margie's crap just forced me to start my own practice sooner than I anticipated. That's all."

"Yeah, the guy who gave us your name told us that she told your bosses and you were asked to resign," Mike said. He leaned back into the booth and looked around to make sure our conversation was still private. It was a habit of his, I noticed.

"That was the rumor, but that's not how it went down obviously. But it doesn't surprise me that people believed the rumor. She's been known to lie to build herself up and make people think she's actually done things she never has. Makes more people fear her." He shrugged.

My mind was racing again. Mike and I had never done anything to Margie. Why put a curse on the items she gave us? It still didn't make any sense.

Mike must have been reading my mind. "Any idea why Margie would have given a complete stranger cursed objects?"

Jack laughed out loud. "Why wouldn't she? She's a sadistic bitch and she likes to control people. Why? She give something to someone?"

"Yeah, she gave it to me," I volunteered.

Jack shook his head. "Well, you're the infamous Liz Tanner. It was probably a power play. She probably bet someone she could control you or wanted to experiment with cursed items and figured you might be a good candidate to play with."

If that was true, that was really awful and Marjorie Ellis needed help. Mental help. All I could manage was, "Wow."

"So she's mentally unstable," Mike prodded.

Jack laughed again. "You can say that again. Whenever anyone even disagreed with her view of something she got aggressive and nasty with them. Threatening even. Not necessarily in what she said, but rather her demeanor."

"Aggressive posture, choice fighting words, that sort of thing?" Mike asked.

The young attorney nodded. "Exactly. Execration magick seems to be a hobby of hers. Pushing other people around, bullying in general, seems to be another. There are two kinds of people in the world. Friends of Marjorie Ellis, and enemies of Marjorie Ellis. My girlfriend and I actually quit the club because of Margie. We didn't feel we were welcome anymore. Though I've heard she's no longer a member because she started her own offshoot group since then. A lot of people there know her though. My guess is most of them probably don't like her."

"The private club?" I asked before Mike had a chance.

"Abyss," Mike clarified.

Jack nodded. "That would be it."

"Reg Mathers told us Margie was still a member." Mike took a swig of his beer. That's when the food arrived and we began eating.

This didn't stop Jack from continuing. "No, I know the head guy over there, Damien Crum. We go golfing sometimes. He isn't a big Margie fan. But you really want to get into her mind and how she works, the woman you need to talk to is Layton. That's her last name. She was Margie's best friend for years. They had a huge falling out and uh, Minerva. Minerva Layton. Real nice lady. Anyway, they had a falling out and I guess Margie cursed her but Minerva is one of those people who resists curses really well. So rumor has it that Margie gave up on cursing her, but it's also part of the reason Margie stopped hanging out at Abyss."

I couldn't help but think of how the magickal community was its own little *Payton Place*. "So Minerva might be able to help us destroy the curse?"

Jack nodded. "Definitely. This isn't the first time she's dealt with Margie and knowing Margie, it's probably not the last. Truces don't last long with that woman. People die around her all the time after they've pissed her off."

"So we've heard," Mike said. This time he sounded uneasy. Even for a skeptic it must have been hard to constantly hear from people who believed in something he didn't believe in. Until now. Eventually he was bound to start doubting his own skepticism when all the people around him were so sure in their convictions and beliefs in the power of curses.

"We've been trying to find out about these cursed objects she gave Liz for a week or more now. It's getting ridiculous." Mike said offhandedly.

"Between you and me, I wouldn't be surprised if she was just using Liz as a test subject for her cursed item *experiment* and if she didn't frame you for that murder because it was another way to show others how much power she has. Probably caught wind you were on to her about her cursed objects. She wanted to get rid of Eric anyway. Right?" Jack went back to eating.

At that point I guessed Mark must have told Jack what was going on since Mike and I hadn't mentioned the murder yet. And Mike had explained it to Mark so that Mark would set up the meeting with Jack. I felt an exasperated sigh cross my lips, unbidden.

"So why not just curse Eric? Let him die of natural causes?" Mike asked.

Jack shrugged. "How did she kill him?"

"Allegedly kill him," Mike corrected. "Police issue revolver, bullet to the back of the head execution style."

"That's heavy. Very pointed, too. Sounds like maybe she was trying to send a message. There's no actual evidence you killed Baca, right?"

Mike shook his head. "It's all circumstantial."

"Well maybe she did that on purpose then. She just wanted to send a message that you were fucking with the wrong woman." Jack ventured.

"I guess that's possible," Mike said. He began biting his lower lip.

We finished lunch, bade Jack goodbye, and headed home. It was another drive in silence with both of us lost in our own thoughts. Mike's brain solving a mystery and mine bitter at Margie and plotting a return curse. Yeah, I know – immature, right? But damn it, no one messes with me and mine and gets away with it! I had every intention of picking Minerva's brain when we met her. I was, at that moment at least, dead set and determined to find a way to give Margie some of her own medicine. Why? Because Karma wasn't working fast enough and quite frankly, I have a really bad temper. At least in my imagination I do.

I was still imagining making poppets of Margie when I heard Mike calling out to me. "Earth to Liz, come in Liz."

Looking around I realized we were home, parked in Mike's driveway. "Oh, we're home. Good."

"Must have been a deep thought," Mike said, obviously hoping I'd let him in on what had taken me so far away that I'd lost track of my surroundings.

"Yeah, it was. I was just plotting revenge," I said with a stoic expression.

Mike started laughing. He knew me better than that. "I look forward to hearing about it."

"No, you don't. It's pretty awful. It involves poppets and curses." I opened the car door and got out.

He followed. "What the hell is a poppet?"

"Effigy," I said without much thought. "Representation of the person you want to hurt."

"Ah, like a voodoo doll," he clarified.

"Something like that. Though the term *voodoo doll* is actually an inappropriate designation." I kind of laughed. I was starting to sound like Mike. Next thing we knew I'd start referring to happenings in my life as *incidents* and those who had wronged me *perpetrators* or *persons-of-interest*. Shaking my head I whispered under my breath, "Designation."

Mike gave me a slight smile and we went inside.

He waited about two hours, leaving me in front of the television with my laptop, before he finally interrupted me. "So Minerva just called me on my cell."

I stopped typing mid-sentence, something I rarely did when I was writing, and set the laptop on the coffee table. "What did she say?"

"She couldn't meet with us this afternoon like planned. But she and Damien Crum are good friends. They want to meet us at *Abyss* tomorrow morning." Mike shrugged and took a swig from the bottle of root beer he was carrying.

"Isn't school in tomorrow? I know it's summer school and all, but still…" I gave Mike a confused look.

He shrugged. "I guess she teaches one class and it's in the early afternoon."

"Minerva, Damien, ugh." I rolled my eyes. "That's fine. At least we're going during the day when their kinky sex dungeon isn't open."

Yeah, it was safe to say I still wasn't warming up to the whole bdsm with spectators thing. At home in the bedroom, that was fine. Public club, private club, didn't matter. And I certainly had no interest in swinging or open relationships. I really hoped Mike was catching my drift.

"Yes, I know you don't like the whole club thing. Just bear with it until we can clear me. Otherwise you'll be visiting me in Cañon City," he said matter-of-fact referring to the Colorado city that was home to nine State prisons and four Federal penitentiaries.

I took a deep breath. Obviously I was willing to endure it for Mike's sake. "Okay," I agreed.

He leaned over and kissed my forehead. "Thanks, babe! Love you!"

And with that he grabbed the newspaper and disappeared into the back bedroom. He knew when it was time to leave me to my writing. Instead, I stared at the glowing computer screen and the blinking cursor for about fifteen minutes. Finally I pulled the laptop off the coffee table and back into my lap and began typing.

The rest of the night was uneventful except for the dreams. Whether they were induced by the stress of our current situation or brought on by divine intervention I suppose I'll never know for sure. I took it as the latter, but only because it lent some insight.

I stood at the edge of a pier that extended at least six hundred yards out into the vast ocean. The ocean, black, was lit by a full moon. In front of me there was a disturbance in the water. The water bubbled up and from the murky depth the serpent began rising. The moonlight glinted against its wet scales. The Leviathan, Dagon. Now don't get me wrong. I know my history of deities. I knew damn well that Dagon was once a god of the land and harvest long before he was worshiped as a fish god. But this was my dream and it was Dagon. He rose above me with the head of a dragon. His eyes weren't black pitch as I somehow expected, but instead they gleamed a brilliant electric blue with a single black slit running through the center.

I wasn't taking such a rare opportunity to seek wisdom from the great serpent for granted, so I immediately took control of the dream, willing my dream self to be an active participant in the dream instead of a passive observer. "Great serpent, I seek your wisdom about the curse and those involved in killing Eric Baca."

Dream me had a very pleasing, booming feminine voice that rose up to the serpent in a grand fashion.

The serpent, Dagon, bent his head toward me. "You know the killer," it told me plainly.

No hissing or raspy voice or anything like that. A pleasing man-voice. My Leviathan serpent Dagon had a very regular man-voice.

That observation aside I took into consideration the serpents words. How come I always had to know the killer? What was so special about me?

Dagon literally groaned. "No, you and Mike know the killer. You should bring a pen."

What? Dream-me scrunched her face in confusion. "Why can't you be direct and not so archaic?"

The serpent laughed. "What fun is that?"

"Any other pearls of wisdom?" Dream-me certainly was good at sounding classy while being sarcastic.

Let me tell you, sarcasm is not lost on Daemons. "Just be careful."

"Thanks, I'll be sure to do that." My heart sank. All the serpent could offer was *be careful?* Admittedly at that moment I found myself really questioning why I even dealt with Daemons sometimes. They seem to have this thing where they expect you to learn your own lessons and figure things out for yourself. I suppose that's not a bad thing overall, but when you need information in a pinch it's a real pain in the ass. You'd almost be better off asking a *Magic 8 Ball*.

I didn't wait for the serpent to disappear and leave me standing alone on the pier. Instead I forced myself to open my eyes only to find myself assaulted by the sunlight pouring through the window. I felt like I hadn't slept a wink.

CHAPTER THIRTEEN
THURSDAY, JULY 6

I wasn't expecting Abyss to be so remote. Nor did I expect the well-kept mansion looming before us. It seemed to take us forever to reach the parking area. I was thankful that Mike had gotten Minerva to help us get an appointment with Damien. We'd kill two birds with one stone this way.

What an awful name, Minerva. I couldn't help but wonder if it was a birth given name or if it was a name she'd chosen for herself. A lot of occultists did that, after all. It was an old tradition, going by a pseudonym; one that I'd never personally gotten into. Sure, I had an alternate online handle, everyone did, but I didn't go by it in the real world. I imagine back when being in a coven was dangerous it was a great idea. No one in the coven knew anyone else's real name, so if one of them squealed it was hard to point fingers. I'm not so sure it has merit in the modern occult world though. It just always seemed so silly to me.

Mostly because everyone is calling him or herself Raven-this or Belladonna-that, or some variation of Nightshade, Phoenix, Willow, Moon-something, Dark-something, Silver-this, something-Wolf, or something with the words *star*, *rune* or *wind* tacked onto it. Online it's even worse because in the *darker* pagan and magickal communities people are constantly adding 666 to the end of their screen names.

Once we were parked we got out. I felt sick to my stomach. This wasn't an ordinary bdsm club in downtown. No, this was an upscale sex-magick cult with enough money behind it to have a remote mansion in the mountains. There was a big difference and I wasn't so sure I was comfortable with such an organized, well-funded group like this one. Not to mention these were all magicians and daemon worshippers that I didn't know, or at least I didn't think I knew them. I know, rare as that is being the public relations front for OTS you'd have thought I knew these people, but I didn't. There were people who were in my circle, and then there were people who didn't draw a lot of attention to themselves.

We walked up the well-kept stone staircase and Mike held the door for me. Much like the small club in Denver, there was a check in station, manned by a bald guy who looked like a pro-wrestler, right inside the door. The guy looked us over as we entered.

"Can I help you?" His voice was just as intimidating as his size.

Mike didn't even flinch. "Yeah, we're here to see Minerva and Damien."

The guy picked up a clipboard from his desk. "Names?"

Without skipping a beat Mike answered, "Mike Katz and Liz Tanner."

The guard's expression lightened up and he looked directly at me. "You're the author of *Daemonic Manifestation*!"

I hope I didn't look as shocked as I felt. I was never good with fans, not face-to-face anyway. I'd never quite mastered the ability to accept compliments or talk about my work without blushing uncontrollably. "Umm, yeah."

"I love that book! My book club is currently reading *Path to the Abyss*. You're one of my favorite writers!" he gushed.

Mike purposefully tapped my hand. I must have looked panic stricken or something, but that tap was enough to get me to respond appropriately. I gave the guard a broad smile, "Well thank you! I'm so happy you enjoy my work."

It wasn't over yet. "Do you think maybe you could autograph some of your books? I have them in my car..."

Of course he did, my inner voice said in a somewhat sarcastic tone. Thank the Daemons Mike stepped in. "Could she sign them on the way out? We don't want to keep Damien and Minerva waiting."

The realization that he was working and still on the clock must have dawned on the guy because he reined himself in. "Oh, uh right. Yeah, that would be great." With that, he got on the phone. Finally he hung up and said, "Minerva will be out to get you in a minute."

With that, he hurried out the door toward the parking lot; probably to get the books.

I was thankful when a tall, thin woman dressed in jeans and a t-shirt stepped out into the lobby, looked around, puzzled, then turned her attention to us.

"He ran out to get some books for Liz to sign on her way out," Mike explained as if reading her mind. "You must be Minerva?"

I would have never guessed the stunning brunette, who looked like Audrey Hepburn from 1950, was a middle school teacher. I would have guessed model or actress. She smiled and nodded. "I am, you must be detective Katz, and we all know Liz. Well, we know of her at least. Come on back," she said, her eyes travelling to the door.

Once she saw the guard coming back up the steps to the front door she ushered us in and closed the door behind us. She looked at me apologetically. "Sorry about that. We don't get a lot of famous authors here. The occasional actor or actress and even a politician now and again, but, well, you know how it is."

Actually I had no clue *how it was*. I was far from being a famous author. The only people who knew about my books were other Daemonolaters. The rest of the world was blissfully unaware of them. I liked it that way. "Yeah, sure," I lied. I threw Mike a shrug and he chuckled causing Minerva to look back at us.

I gave her a bright smile, or what I hoped was bright. For all I knew I looked like a *Chucky doll*, but she didn't flinch away or anything like that so I imagined my facial expression was just fine. Or I hoped it was. I was often accused of being angry or sad when I was neither. I guess I don't have one of those good expression faces.

We continued to follow Minerva through a maze of abandoned rooms, some containing what I recognized as dungeon equipment. Yes, I'd done some internet research, so I knew bdsm equipment when I saw it. She led us through several long hallways; one painted black and two painted deep red. Finally, we reached our destination. It was a large office with oak paneling and an entire sitting area replete with high back chairs. The bookcases along the walls were filled with books about sex magick and the occult. I really hoped nothing bad happened because there was no way Mike and I would find our way out of the maze that was *Abyss*.

Mike must have noticed my uneasiness because he put a protective arm around me. To the left stood at a massive oak desk. Behind the desk sat a man who I assumed was Damien. He dyed his hair black. Sure, I may not be a girly girl, but I could spot a dye job a mile off. Damien was on the phone, though I wondered if he was pretending just to exaggerate his importance.

Minerva motioned to the two chairs sitting strategically facing the desk. "Have a seat. Can I get either of you something to drink?"

I shook my head, still taking in the room. Mike said something but I wasn't listening. Instead, I found my eyes traveling the walls of the room from one painting to another. The artwork was grand and dark and impressively framed. I would have loved some art like that for my house. My heart sank. I no longer had a house and I'd lost most of my paintings to the tornado. Still, the work was magnificent. A lot of it detailed. I was so entranced by the work that I didn't realize the other people in the room were all watching me wander from painting to painting, inspecting each one.

"You like art?" Damien asked.

"I was a bit of a collector myself," I said, stopping at a four foot tall painting of Baphomet, remembering the small black and white Baphomet painting that used to hang in my bathroom.

"Was?"

"Uh huh. My house got hit by a tornado earlier this week. Most of my paintings were lost with the house." I moved on to the next painting, enjoying the physique of the Daemonic male figure holding a scourge.

"Which brings us to why we've asked for this meeting," Mike added.

Damien, who was now standing, obviously uncomfortable with the fact that we weren't sitting, nodded. "Minerva told me what you talked about on the phone. Cursed objects. Did you bring them?"

"Hell no," I blurted. "We put them someplace safe where no one can get their hands on them. They were in my house and it was taken out by a tornado. Carrying them around would be certain suicide."

"I see. And you think Marjorie Ellis is behind this?" Damien said.

I noticed Minerva's lack of participation in the conversation. Then it dawned on me that she probably was a submissive. "I know she's behind the cursed objects. But there's more to it than that."

"Ah, yes. Murder." At that point, Damien turned to Mike. "So you think Marjorie Ellis framed you for murder because?"

"Because she hated her ex and she knew Liz and I were looking for her regarding her cursed objects," Mike said.

Damien nodded. "Kill two birds with one stone. That sounds like Margie. Get rid of the ex and frame the people asking too many questions about extra-curricular activities. I'm following you."

Mike nodded. "Exactly. So we need to find her. She's incredibly elusive and no one seems to know where she is. We were told both of you used to be friends of hers. That she was in your inner circle. Maybe you know where she's at?"

Minerva wore a crooked smile. She finally said, "Yeah, right now we're probably not the people to talk to. Marjorie stopped coming here after she was booted from our inner circle. If anything, she's probably cursing us, too."

"Well, if she's capable of killing someone and framing me for it, then she's obviously dangerous," Mike said.

I knew better. Mike knew better, but he was banking on them viewing Marjorie as a personal threat to them.

Damien nodded again and gave Minerva a worried glance. Letting out a sigh he said, "We think Margie still has informants within the limited membership of Abyss. I find it suspicious that she knows about all our activities and rituals. It's a matter of finding out who those people are. We won't be able to do it."

"We could come in undercover and try to find her informants and get information from them on how to find her," Mike suggested thoughtfully.

I opened my mouth to protest, but nothing came out. Instead I thought about clearing Mike, and really, that's all that mattered at the moment. Instead I said, "If we go in asking about Margie people are going to be suspicious."

A sly grin slid over Minerva's face. "Yes, but there is a way to do it. It's just that you're going to need to become visitors to the club - from out of town. You're not Liz Tanner and Mike Katz. No, you're Janet Lane and Bruce Perry visiting from Portland, and as it turns out, our rituals are a bit too tame for you."

"I don't follow," I admitted.

"Well obviously you're both into the scene. Some sex magick groups keep it classy. We're one of them. One of Marjorie's biggest complaints is we don't allow knife play or rape role-playing during sex magick ritual."

I realized my jaw was hanging open and forced it closed. "Mike and I are…"

"Willing to go with that story line," Mike finished.

I gave him a brief scowl but gave in. *It's to clear Mike of a murder charge*, I silently scolded myself.

Damien and Minerva seemed confused by my reaction.

"We don't usually do the whole public play thing. We keep our sex magick behind closed doors," he explained.

"Ah," Damien nodded respectfully. "Well, I am afraid Minerva is correct. The only way to get anyone to give you any information would be to pretend to be from out of town here on business or vacation and looking for stronger rituals than ours. If you want our little group to believe your criticism of our ritual, it means you'll actually have to attend one, openly criticize it, and hope one of Margie's cronies takes the bait, pulls you aside and gives you some contact information," Damien concluded, then added, "All I ask is you tell me who the informants are so I know where my information leak is."

"There's only one problem." I smiled at them and didn't wait for a response. "Your front door guy knows who we are and is *my number one fan.*"

Damien laughed. "I'll handle Mitch."

"Thank you." I gave him the best smile I could manage.

"So when is the next ritual?" Mike asked.

"I know time is of the essence in this instance so you have two choices," Damien started. There was a knock at the door.

Minerva hurried to the door, opened it a crack and peered out, but whoever was on the other side was stronger and wanted to see Damien. In walked Reg Mathers.

Reg gave Minerva a frown, then looked at Damien, then at us. His expression gave way to confusion. "What are you two doing here?"

"Talking to Damien," Mike said, again without skipping a beat. That confidence of his astounded me sometimes. I would never have the guts to walk into just any situation like I was in complete control.

Reg sauntered across the room and took a chair. "Can the rest of you excuse us? Damien and I have some things to discuss."

Again, Mike and I exchanged glances then looked at our hosts.

Damien nodded at us. "Could you guys give us a minute?"

Minerva opened the door and disappeared into the hallway. Mike and I followed and I closed the door behind me

The door was thick and the walls were thick, too. Despite that we were able to hear muffled, raised voices.

"Would you both like some coffee? A cold beverage maybe?" Minerva offered with a nervous glance to Damien's office door. She didn't wait for an answer. "Follow me."

We followed back down the hallway from where we'd come and into a small room on the right. It was a small kitchen-like area sans stove or oven. It was simply some cupboards, a sink, a refrigerator, a microwave, there was a coffee maker on the counter and there was a table and four chairs.

None of us helped ourselves to the chairs.

Minerva, still nervous, opened the fridge. "I have water, green tea, Frappuccino, and Pepsi."

"I'll have water," I said. I figured I ought to be polite and take something.

Mike shook his head. "No, I'm fine thank you."

He was biting his lip so I knew his brain was in *detective* mode. Why was Reg here? I wondered. Then common sense smacked me upside the head. Was it really any of our business? After all, the Daemonolatry community was relatively small. The sex magick community within that community was even smaller. It stood to reason everyone knew everyone and that's exactly why I was beginning to think this whole plan of pretending to be from out of town was stupid. Even if people didn't know me in the flesh, they knew my name. Luckily I didn't have a profile on any social networking websites with a real picture of me so I did retain some anonymity, but still - I was not going to trust that. It was with that last thought that I became acutely aware of eyes on me.

I looked up.

Minerva and Mike were looking at me. Minerva held out the water.

I took it with a sheepish grin. "Thanks."

"It's that writer brain. Liz sometimes goes off into her own little world," Mike told Minerva with a grin.

If Minerva hadn't been standing there I would have reached out and smacked him for such a snarky comment. Of course he was still bigger than me and playful smacks often begot playful spankings.

A popular pop song began blaring from Minerva's hip. She clicked her phone out of its holder and answered, "Minerva Fox."

Did she really have to use a fake name? I caught myself smiling and fought the urge to roll my eyes. Minerva Layton at least sounded real and undoubtedly her last name really was Layton. Minerva Fox sounded like porn star. I stopped mid-thought and didn't follow said thought to its logical, or perhaps prudish, conclusion.

The conversation on her end consisted of a series of "Uh huh.", "Yeah.", and "Alright" and concluded with a "Okay, I'll see you then." She hung up and gave us an apologetic smile. "Sorry about that."

Just then we heard footfalls pass through the hall outside.

Minerva's phone went off again. This time it looked like she was checking a text message. "Ah, looks like Damien is ready for us again."

We followed her again as she led us back to Damien's office. When we entered, Damien looked stressed out.

"Where were we?" he started.

"Planning on making sure your guy up front wouldn't rat us out if we attend the next rite to phish for Margie's private group information, and you were about to give us the date and time for the ritual," Mike said. He didn't stop there. "What was Reg Mathers doing here if you don't mind me asking?"

Damien lifted an eyebrow and set his jaw. It was so obvious he was hiding something, but it probably wasn't any of our concern. "He's a former group member. He and I had some business."

I cringed on the inside, waiting for Mike to overstep his boundaries again, but he didn't.

"Sorry for prying," Mike said instead. "It's just that we've been dealing with Reg and he's been helpful. Maybe too helpful. I don't know."

Damien nodded. "Well, he's no friend of Marjorie's either, so that actually makes sense."

"Ah." Mike started chewing his lip again.

"Next ritual is tomorrow night at seven-fifteen sharp. Show up early for cocktails. A drink or two might help you both relax if you're uncomfortable with the group scene." Damien forced a smile.

I smiled back at him and Mike did likewise. Then, with as much flair and muster, Minerva led us from the office and toward the front of the building again.

"Don't worry too much about Damien. He's always a bit gruff like that," she told us.

"He seemed agitated after Reg left," Mike said matter-of-fact.

"He and Reg don't always see eye-to-eye," she said with a note of caution.

Mike nodded. "I got that."

We reached the door leading out into the lobby with the guard station. "Well it was great to meet you both and I look forward to seeing you tomorrow night." She shook both our hands and when she took mine she added, "I'll make you an extra stiff drink. It's not all that bad."

I nodded politely. "Thank you. We'll see you then."

She gave us a polite nod and turned and left while Mike led me back into the lobby.

As we left I paused at Mitch, who had a stack of every book I'd ever written sitting at his guard station.

"I really appreciate you signing these for me Ms. Tanner," he said in a half whisper. "I swear no one will find out who you are. Damien explained everything."

"I really appreciate that, Mitch," I said. "If the circumstances were different I'd tell you that you could call me Liz. But, well..." I shrugged.

He nodded. "I completely understand, Ms. Lane. I look forward to seeing you and Mr. Perry tomorrow night."

Damien sure hadn't wasted any time explaining the details to Mitch. I wondered when he had time.

Mike sat patiently waiting for me to finish signing the stack of books. Ten minutes later I was done. I handed Mitch's pen back to him. "Here you go."

"Thanks!" He started scooping books off the counter and putting them back into the duffel bag he kept them in.

"You're welcome," I said with a smile, then turned and followed Mike out the door and into the parking lot.

As we neared the car Mike suddenly turned to me. "Did any of *that* seem strange to you?"

"Which part, Mike?" I laughed. The *'did that seem strange'* question was becoming a part of our normal routine. "That entire meeting seemed strange to me. Like everyone was holding back, and what's up with that Mitch guy? Not to mention how did Mitch already know everything by the time we reached the door?"

Mike just shook his head and unlocked the car with a click of his keyless remote. "There was something not quite right about that whole thing, Ms. Lane."

I got into the car. "I guess you'll have to explain it to me over dinner, Mr. Perry. Or do you prefer Sherlock?"

"Sarcasm. Ouch. Let's grab something on the road and take it home." He started the car and we pulled from the parking lot.

For whatever reason I felt a lot better once we were back on the interstate heading home.

CHAPTER FOURTEEN
FRIDAY, JULY 7

My night as Janet Lane started earlier in the day with me calling Minerva to ask her what the dress code was. The latex dress and spike heels seemed cheap somehow and inappropriate for what was, for all intents and purposes, a spiritual rite. I was glad I called because evidently this was a chic crowd. Minerva was quick to suggest a black cocktail dress for me and a pair of dress slacks and a button down shirt for Mike. Of course all of that would be removed before the ritual, at which point the participants got to choose whether to go skyclad or robed, she told me. Then she went on to add that if we wore robes we'd be expected to be nude underneath. Expected? Was someone going to check? While the prospect of that made me nervous I went about putting together our necessary attire. While I owned several black cowl hooded robes, unfortunately my wardrobe didn't include a cocktail dress. I begrudgingly found myself with Alyssa at the mall going through the racks at some small party dress boutique.

I looked into the mirror, deciding all of the dresses I'd tried on looked awful on my frumpy frame. "This isn't going to work," I whined.

Alyssa's arm, holding yet another black dress, entered the dressing room. "Quit your damn whining and put this one on."

"Thanks for the sympathy." I grabbed the dress out of her hand and hung it on the hook. I began taking off the ugly one I had on. "You're tall and gorgeous. I'm short and plain. These dresses make me look unattractive."

"It's not you," she said from outside the door. "It's the dresses. Most women's clothing is designed by gay men and they don't account for women who have curves. They make dresses for women shaped like fourteen-year-old boys." There was a note of disgust in her voice.

I groaned and put on cocktail dress number four. It had a low plunging V-neck, it hugged my curves, and it hit me about mid-thigh. I shrugged at myself in the mirror. It wasn't too bad. "This one doesn't suck," I finally admitted aloud.

"Let me see!" Alyssa's voice had that girly ring of excitement in it.

I opened the dressing room door and stepped out.

Alyssa's face froze for a second and then a huge smile spread over her lips. "That, my dear, is absolutely smokin' hot on you. Good gods, Mike is going to have to fight to keep his hands to himself."

I groaned. "Let's pick another one."

"Wait! Why?" She placed both hands firmly on her hips. If I didn't know any better I would have thought I was two inches from being smacked.

"I don't want men ogling me just before a sex magick rite knowing I'll be naked under my robes."

She began laughing and shook her head. "You'll be with Mike. Men like it when people look at their woman. They get that 'She's with me and not you jackass' smugness about them. It's an ego boost. Mike could use one. You don't actually think he's going to let anyone near you, do you?"

"He let Reg Mathers near me." I looked back at myself in the full length mirror. The dress did look good on me.

Alyssa sighed then reminded me, "The Reg thing was different. He had to get in good with that guy for information."

"I'm sure there were other ways to do that."

"Still pissed at him for..."

I stopped her mid-sentence by holding up my hand and looking around to make sure the sales associates couldn't overhear. "That was completely humiliating. You have no idea."

"But that's what's exciting about it," she shot back without missing a beat. "You clearly aren't getting the whole dominance submission thing."

"Oh no, I get it," I assured her. "I'm just not into the exhibitionism or humiliation *thing*. At home in the bedroom - great. Out in public, not so much."

"Fair enough. However," she took another glowing look at the dress, "This is a higher class of people you're dealing with, so I don't think they're going to invite themselves to play with another man's woman. It would probably be considered presumptuous and even rude. Kind of like how in swordsmanship and gunmanship clubs you always ask if you can touch another man's weapon."

Alyssa certainly had an interesting way of putting things. I had no choice but to relent. "I'll get the dress."

She clapped her hands together. "Yay!"

I laughed and shook my head. Leave it to me to have the only perky blonde, cheerleading (metaphorically speaking) Satanist in existence as my bff. With that thought

I closed the door, took off the dress, and got back into my street clothes.

●

People were very polite. Mike and I were sitting in the Abyss antechamber sipping drinks and no one was any the wiser to who we were or why we were there. To them, we really were Janet Lane and Bruce Perry, two practitioners from out of town, just visiting. We were met with warm hellos and kind gestures and it didn't seem like there was a mean-spirited person in the bunch. None of them seemed to be gawking at us or looking at either of us as pieces of meat. It was hard to believe any of them were, firstly, into bdsm sex magick, and secondly playing double agent for Margie. Then again, it could have been someone who was innocent and by innocent I mean one of those people who thinks they can be neutral friends with two people who are at odds with one another. But really, people like that can turn out to be shit-stirrers even though they don't seem underhanded at all. I wasn't sure I would be able to criticize their sex magick technique. After all – these people weren't here for the sex. It was very clear to me they were actually here for the sex magick. Judging by the conversations I was overhearing this was a hardcore group. They were all about the magick. Butterflies began fluttering in my stomach.

Mike must have noticed something was up. He immediately gave me an inquisitive look and led me to the side of the room where no one could overhear. "What's wrong? You look like you've had a vision."

I shook my head. "No, but I don't think these people are going to buy that we don't think they're hardcore enough. This is going to be a tough crowd."

Mike looked around. "Why do you say that?"

"They know their magick, Mike. That's really the primary reason most of them are here. These aren't people looking for an excuse to have an orgy."

Mike bit his lip. "So how are we going to play this?"

I shrugged. "We'll have to play it by ear. Of course we might find their ritual too tame. Or I'll find some other aspect to critique that I think Margie might be more into."

"That sounds like winging it babe." Mike let out a nervous laugh.

"It is," I said with a quick grin. "But if there's one subject I know intimately, it's magick. So we're safe."

Just then someone hit the gong standing next to the doors leading into the ritual chamber. I jumped.

A tall, thin man with a shaved head stood next to the door and announced in a deep voice, "The rite will commence in fifteen minutes if everyone would please take this time to don your formal robes or to remove your attire completely."

My stomach did a somersault. Both Mike and I had brought our formal robes and earlier had stowed them in the *his and her* dressing room lockers provided us. I pretended to know what I was doing and followed several women into the ladies changing area. I smiled politely when I was acknowledged and went to my locker, not averting my eyes from my task of changing.

"What was your name again?" One of the women next to me asked.

"Janet, Janet Lane," I said quickly with a courteous smile.

"I'm Jessica." She held out her hand.

I politely took it and gave her a warm handshake. "It's nice to make your acquaintance."

"So how do you find our group so far?"

"Much more formal and organized than I'm used to," I said.

She nodded. "We're told that a lot. You know, a lot of these groups that practice sex magick, it's all about the sex. But we have created some powerful servitors with these rites. We generally involve them in politics."

I fought back a surprised smile. "Sex magick is definitely potent for that. So is there going to be any pain or torture?" I asked, a bit nervous.

Jessica laughed and the woman next to her chimed in, "No, if you want that sort of thing you have to find your way into the private, invite only rituals."

Jessica shrugged. "I don't know, Colleen, Damien and Minerva did do that knife play session last year."

"Yeah, but it's not like we do that sort of thing all the time," the woman named Colleen told Jessica. Then she leaned around Jessica toward me, "Tonight we're really just feeding our servitors. We do that at least once a month."

I nodded, not really sure what to say. "Feeding servitors is pretty tame."

Jessica nodded. "Yeah, it is. But if you're really wanting knife play or even faux non-consensual I can put you in contact with a small group of people here who do *that* independent of this group."

"I might be interested," I said, hoping I didn't sound overly eager. The last thing I wanted was these people thinking I was some sort of masochist and Mike a sadist. Though it was probably too late for that. Even though the people she was talking about were here, maybe they knew Margie.

"Dear, for knives and heavy whipping, caning, and extreme bondage you want Margie," another woman said. Dressed in black leather everything and wearing bright red lipstick, she produced a card and handed it to me. "They really know how to throw a sadist rite. There's a great deal of power in pain."

"Thanks," I said, taking the card.

There was a span of silence as the unnamed Domme slipped out of her sexy ensemble and strode from the room completely naked. Of course she had the body to pull it off.

Being the prude I am, I undressed to my underwear, slipped my robe on over my head, and removed my underclothes under cover. That's when I realized Jessica was looking at me with a great deal of concern.

"Do me a favor," she started, waiting to get eye contact with me. When she got it she said, "Don't call the number on that card. The woman Karen just referred you to is evil."

Colleen scoffed, straightening the hood of her robe. "Not evil as in evil, but like – a total bitch who would stab you in the back. Not to mention their rituals are sick. They actually hire phlebotomists to come draw vials of blood from ritual participants, add it all to a bowl and then everyone is anointed with the blood, or made to drink it."

"I heard they blackmail young virgins into giving up their virginity in the name of Asmodeus. Like take nude pictures of them and then threaten to show the pictures to parents or bosses. That sort of thing. During the rituals they pour blood on them before they rape them on the altar, then severely cane them," Jessica whispered, looking really concerned.

My stomach turned. "Yikes."

"Yeah, it's really bad. We should go, four minutes," Jessica said. She and Colleen both smiled sweetly at me and left the room, leaving me standing there.

Without a second glance, I slipped Margie's card in my messenger bag along with my bra and panties and zipped it up, then closed the locker door. It appeared Mike and I wouldn't have to criticize the ritual after all, though the fact that we still had to participate in the ritual gave me cause to not be as cheery as I wanted to be. As I left the changing room to join Mike, I reminded myself to tell Damien and Minerva that Karen, who exuded a great deal of nasty energy in my opinion, was most definitely their leak to Margie.

Mike was standing in the hallway outside the antechamber waiting for me. I motioned him close. "I got a card with Margie's info."

"Really?"

I nodded. "Yep. I guess we need to follow."

We began walking forward, through the antechamber to the tall oak doors leading into the actual ritual chamber. We were the last ones inside and behind us the tall bald man closed the door. We followed those around us and stood at the outer edge of the circle. Evidently we were standing in the quadrant of fire judging by the seal of Asmodeus beneath my feet. It felt like sacrilege to be standing there, but clearly it's what we were supposed to be doing. I tried to never walk on seals. I felt it was bad manners, but it's what everyone else was doing. I looked down to make sure others were standing on seals, too. They were. *When in Rome*, I immediately thought.

Another gong sounded from the east side of the room. That's when I realized the altar was backlit and the sigil of Lucifer, the one from the *Grand Grimoire*, stood out stark white against the black wall. The altar itself was outfitted with two fine ornate silver chalices, a sleek ritual blade, and a black leather scourge.

If anything it was theatrical. The high priest, wearing a black hood, but no shirt and black pants, approached the altar. He looked more like an executioner than a presiding priest. *BDSM sex magick cult*, I gently reminded myself. He began by intoning the Enn of Lilith and worked his way, with a staff in hand, around the circle clockwise conjuring Daemons of fire and lust.

A shadow about the size of a couch moved above me and I looked up, surprised by what I saw. Above me hovered the largest servitor I'd ever seen. These guys weren't kidding. They did, in fact, have a very large servitor and keeping it fed took a great deal of energy.

It swooped over head again then seemed to rest above the seal of Venus, like a dog politely waiting for its supper. It didn't really have a shape, but it was a semi-opaque mass of shadow, and when it moved you could feel it pass because the air moved with it. I looked over at Mike. His eyes were huge. Evidently he was seeing the same thing. I imagine it was the first time he'd ever seen a servitor.

Admittedly I was a lazy magician in that I used servitors now and again, but unlike some folks, I never kept one around permanently for the same reason I didn't have pets. They required time and attention that I didn't really have to give.

I looked around the ritual chamber again, taking in the vast amount of stimuli and noticing new things. The center of the room was set stage-like with a table covered in what appeared to be soft cushions. *That must be where the sex happens* my inner-voice chimed in. There was also one of those Saint Andrew Crosses, like those I'd seen on the Internet, to the side of that.

Once the priest finished making his way around the circle and the Daemonic was sufficiently called upon, the priest motioned for the gong to sound again. From a doorway hidden by black curtains on the opposite side of the room, a nude, rope bound and blindfolded woman was led by two cloaked figures to the table in the center of the room. There, they restrained her, leaving her legs splayed open so the priests could have their way with her.

The writhing mass above Venus pulsated a little in anticipation and the energy of the room changed. The male participants, I imagine, were very aroused by the beautiful woman lying nude before them. One of the robed figures approached her again, this time with a quill and a bottle of ink. He began vibrating the words of the Seal of the Opener and drew the Seal on her stomach.

My jaw dropped in surprise. I quickly closed my mouth, not wanting anyone to realize I was gawking. I'd never considered the possibility that they'd be having intercourse with a woman channeling the Daemonic. It gave me a whole new appreciation for the notion of sex with Daemons. Before this I really did think that incubi and succubi were silly and childish fantasies. Once again I had been proven wrong.

When the seal was complete, the Enn of Astarte was read over her.

"The vessel of Astarte is ready," one of the priests proclaimed in a loud, deep voice.

Then the priests surrounded her, penises erect, and one-by-one they took turns mounting her until each of them had reached orgasm. That's when it occurred to me there were couples all around us doing their own thing and we were standing in the midst of what appeared to be an orgy of sacred lust. Mike and I stood frozen, completely out of place, for about fifteen minutes as a skrying session took place in center-ring. About five minutes after that the moans of desire finally began to wane. No one seemed to notice we weren't participating. I wasn't going to complain, though I was a bit upset the distraction and noise had caused me to miss the skrying, which remained between the woman channeling Astarte and the priests around her. Not that I would have been able to hear anyway.

The shadowy mass above us had grown and slowed to a methodic pulse. In reverse order the priest closed the ritual, the gong sounded and before we knew it, the entire group, including us, had filed out of the ritual chamber and back into the antechamber where wine and martinis were being served.

I grabbed a glass of wine and downed it.

Mike handed me another. "Maybe you should have gone for the martini?"

I didn't say anything. My mind was still on the ritual and how the young woman became a portal for the Daemon. The servitor was a big one, too. I wondered then what would happen if something that big got away from its keepers. What kind of havoc or destruction could it wreak?

Minerva approached us, pulling me out of my formal dissection of the ritual.

"So what did you think? Did you both enjoy yourselves?" She looked at each of us expectantly.

"The ritual was brilliant, but in other news, we found your leak," I said with a satisfied smile.

Minerva's eyebrows raised in surprise. "That was quick."

"I found out before the ritual."

"Who is it?" Minerva asked, moving closer to me to ensure our conversation stayed between us.

"It's Karen," I whispered.

Minerva's left eyebrow rose. She knew exactly who I meant. I could see it in her eyes. "I should have known."

"Yeah, she does give off that vibe," I agreed.

"Damien is not going to like this," she said with a sigh.

"On a brighter note," I started, trying to lighten the mood, "I really enjoyed the ritual. I'm actually very interested in the technique of the channeling construct. It's too bad I didn't get to hear more of the divination session."

Minerva's expression softened and her eyes lit up, "Oh I know – brilliant, right? I imagine the channeling was about current political affairs. That's both Damien and Lars' current passion at the moment. They're attempting to effect politics with the servitor." She shook her head.

Mike laughed. "I would really like to know how it turns out." He looked at me then. "We need one of those to keep you and I out of trouble."

Both Minerva and I laughed, then Minerva moved off to find Damien to, I suppose, tell him about their leak.

We ran into Jessica, the woman from the dressing room, and her husband, Bill. She was a real estate agent, he owned a car dealership. Of course Mike and I couldn't tell anyone who we really were so we stuck to our story that I was Janet Lane, a manager at a department store, and Mike was Bruce Perry, a high level executive in the packing industry; both jobs that sounded boring as hell so we figured no one would be interested in hearing about them. We were right. No one wanted to dwell on the topic of our jobs for long. Mostly people wanted to talk magick and Daemons – both topics I was perfectly comfortable with. Mike let me do most of the talking.

After four glasses of wine, three too many, I found myself redressing in the ladies changing room, and then alongside Mike saying farewell to our hosts and finally, in the car. I pulled out the business card stashed in my bag.

Mike had one martini and drank water the rest of the night, so he was driving. "So we'll call Gary tomorrow and give him the address and have him run it for us."

I looked at the card. It had a black silk finish and the lettering was in silver. I read it aloud in a boisterous voice, "Marjorie and Lawrence, The Path of the Scourge, Infernal Asmodai! Three-three-twelve Grant Street."

"That's in the warehouse district." Mike eased onto the highway, merging seamlessly with the late night traffic on I-70 eastbound. "We'll plan that for tomorrow night."

A mental tug quickly informed me that going to the warehouse was a bad idea, but I knew there was no way to convince Mike otherwise. We were going whether the Daemons warned us against it or not.

That night I had nightmares. I don't know if they were alcohol induced or sparked by my gut feelings, but in the dreams I was being chased by someone or something. I couldn't see who or what it was. I woke up several times in a cold sweat. Each time I woke up, the more difficult it became to fall back asleep. By the time the first light of morning came through the window I gave up trying and wandered into the kitchen for an aspirin. My head pounded with the hangover from the night before.

CHAPTER FIFTEEN
SATURDAY, JULY 8

Alleyways aren't really my favorite place. At ten o'clock at night they're just downright scary. Especially the ones in the warehouse district just Northeast of Denver. Maybe I've seen one too many episodes of *Law & Order*. All I know is that's where we ended up and we went late because, naturally, Mike wanted to poke around in the dark. We parked and got out. Mike seemed to know exactly where he was going and allegedly Gary was on his way as backup. The fact that we needed backup sent my stomach into knots. The hot air from another ninety-three degree day of mountain desert heat held that faint, sickly smell of oil and paper; oil from the trucks that delivered to the warehouses and paper from the paper mill across the street.

Once we got to a particular ally Mike flashed the light from his flashlight on all the doors leading into warehouses on either side. When the beam of light fell on it I grabbed his arm. "There."

"Daemonic sigil," he agreed. He'd been studying.

"Sigil of Asmodeus," I elaborated, recognizing the identifying *tail* on the Solomonic Daemon sigil.

"The Daemon of lust who keeps showing up everywhere, including my house?"

"Who else? It's a sex magick cult, who'd you expect?" I asked with a shrug.

He nodded. "That makes sense." He took a step toward the door and touched the sigil.

"Eww, gross, don't touch that!" I reached into my jacket and pulled out some liquid spray hand sanitizer and urged him to spray some on his fingers.

"Why?"

"Menstrual blood and paint."

That was enough for Mike. He grabbed the sanitizer out of my hand and pumped the sprayer five times in one hand then vigorously rubbed his hands together. "Ugh."

"Yeah," I agreed.

A loud bang resounded through the ally causing us both to jump, and we heard a fierce meow and hissing. My heart was pounding in my chest. Damn cats. I looked back toward Mike to find he'd already opened the door and was getting ready to step inside.

"Mike, what are you doing?" I could hear the panic in my own voice.

"It's unlocked. I'm going inside, come on." With a fearless bravado I was convinced only cops possessed, he walked into the building, urging me to follow.

I felt a great deal of reluctance, but I found myself tip toeing right behind him. The scent of incense mingled with candle wax assaulted my nose. Of course the inside of the warehouse was dimly lit, but we heard voices and saw the soft glow of red light from up ahead. It looked like they'd hung curtains to partition off different areas. I grabbed Mike's arm, causing him to stop. "Let's go," I mouthed. I was scared. Not that I'm usually a big chicken, but I was having flashbacks to when that crazy bitch, Allison Myers, the rogue occult crime investigator, tried to kill me three months earlier. For whatever reason this situation had the same feeling to it. If I had to choose between going to jail for a murder I didn't commit, or being murdered, I'd pick jail.

He shook his head and pulled out his gun. Then he motioned me to follow.

I gulped at the lump in my throat. Why couldn't we have just waited for Gary? He said he'd be coming.

There was a noise next to me me and a click and a man's voice said from the darkness to my right, "Drop it or the bitch takes a bullet to the head."

Mike lifted his hands in surrender, his fingers visible and nowhere near the trigger or trigger guard. Two more men with guns appeared. The taller blond took Mike's gun. "Who the fuck are you and what are you doing here?"

"We're looking for Marjorie," I heard myself say. I could feel the guy next to me; his aura or something. I was also acutely aware of the gun pointed right above my ear.

"With a gun? Let me guess, you're not friends?" the guy deadpanned.

"I know how this looks," Mike started. "We know she had something to do with Eric Baca's death. The gun was only precautionary."

"Eric Baca?" the tall blond repeated. "You can talk to Larry. Come with us. I'll keep this." He tucked Mike's gun in his jacket.

The guy next to me pushed me forward by the shoulder and Mike and I followed the men toward the light to one of the curtained off areas. There, sitting in a chair smoking a pipe sat a man with long brown hair and goatee. He wasn't wearing a shirt and a Levi's Baphomet was tattooed on his left shoulder. There was a red inverse pentagram on his chest.

"Which one of you assholes forgot to lock the back door again?" When none of the men jumped up to take blame, Larry (I assumed it was Larry, or Lawrence according to the business card) shook his head. "Brent, go lock the back door."

The guy behind me immediately started back the way we came and I sighed with relief knowing his gun was no longer pointed at my head.

"I'm Lawrence Black and you are?"

If it weren't for our precarious situation, I assure you I would have fallen to the floor in fits of laughter. These people were so stereotypical it was pathetic, but they also had guns. Guns win hands down and they're not particularly funny.

"Mike and Liz," Mike said in a flat tone, clearly not willing to give any more information than that.

"So what can I do for you, Mike and Liz?"

"What do you know about Eric Baca?" Mike asked.

Larry looked genuinely confused. "Never heard of him."

One of the women sitting quietly on the couch got up and whispered something in Larry's ear.

He cocked his head as if considering this new information. "I've been informed my woman used to date a guy named Eric Baca."

"Well see, that's why we're here. Turns out he got murdered and me, along with my girlfriend here, are being framed for it. Of course the problem with that is we didn't do anything."

Larry shrugged and grinned. "How's that my problem?"

"We think your group had a hand in it."

"You have proof of that?"

"No, but I have some cursed objects."

"They're not cursed," came a woman's voice from the left. Marjorie stepped out of the darkness. "They're bonded. Big difference. Well, initially I had cursed them, but

I decided later to bond them. Then I just decided to give them away because it occurred to me he'd never take them back. Eric knew me well enough to guess what I'd done." She shrugged.

"So you gave me bonded objects knowingly..." I felt my voice trail off. That was a huge no-no in the Daemonolatry world. You didn't give someone a bonded object unless your intentions were nefarious.

She smiled and shook her head as if to say, stupid girl. "You two are quite convenient. You," she pointed at me, "Are far too sensitive for your own good. When you felt the residual energy from the curses off the items and you started poking your noses into the items and into my life, well, I couldn't have that. So I merely sent some curses through them to get you both to stop. You're both very stubborn."

"And you're a bitch," I took a step toward her only to find Mike's arm holding me back.

What the hell did she mean we were convenient? My mind raced. Mike and I exchanged glances.

That's when it hit me. "Wait, so you knowingly gave me bonded objects without my consent, sent nasty vibes through the damn thing so we'd quit snooping around, then when we didn't stop trying to find out how to remove the, what we thought were curses, you figured you'd use us to your advantage so we would seek out Eric to take off the alleged curse, so you'd have someone to frame for murder? Or maybe you were hoping we'd give him some of the stuff and you could then curse him through them." They were the only explanations that made sense. "You framed us! Maybe you even planned it from the beginning."

A surprised look passed over Mike's face. Either I'd said something he hadn't considered or he was surprised I was mouthing off to the people with the guns.

"No, I can't say I take that kind of credit. To be honest I didn't plan on framing you. Not initially. You just ended up being convenient when I found out you were digging." She shrugged again. "Of course I never really expected you to have enough time to come after me."

I found myself at a loss for words. "Wait, how did you know what we were doing?"

"I have a friend who's a seer who used the bonded objects to watch you guys. They only need to be in close proximity to you for her to see what you were up to."

"So you were watching us the whole time."

She nodded. "Afraid so."

That made sense and it explained so much. It was my turn to bite my lip as I put it all together. *Centrally located my ass*, I thought, remembering how Margie had told me she wanted to give me the items to get rid of because I was more *centrally located* - and here she had moved to Denver. I felt used and stupid.

"But you haven't heard the best part," Margie said with a wide grin. "While I had considered framing you both for murder, I never had a chance to do anything to Eric. You see, Eric wasn't sweet and innocent. I'm sure you've both heard about what a bitch I am. Well, Eric was a bigger jerk than me. The asshole was planning on outing me at work and with my family if I didn't pay him five hundred bucks a month. That's why I had to move out of my house and why I moved back to Denver and now live with Larry. So there you go. I didn't kill Eric and technically I wasn't the one who framed you."

"Then who did?" Mike's face showed no visible signs of emotion.

She shrugged. "Probably someone else he was blackmailing. I'm sure I wasn't the only one. Eric was a bit opportunistic like that. He got what he deserved though."

"You do realize conspiracy to murder someone is a crime, right? So is conspiracy to frame a police officer, or anyone else, for murder."

Mike was pissed. I could tell by the look on his face. My stomach was in knots. "Who else would he have been blackmailing?"

Marjorie shrugged again and gave Mike a nervous look.

"Liz, just don't believe her. She's lying. She's the one who framed us. She admitted it. Now she's backtracking and trying to blame it on someone else." Mike shook his head and looked at Marjorie again.

The entire time, Larry sat quietly listening to the conversation. Finally, it was his turn to say something. "Well, we have to kill them."

"What?" It escaped my lips before I had time to stop it.

Mike said nothing and continued to glare at Marjorie.

"Are *you* going to kill them?" Margie looked at Larry, obviously annoyed.

Larry rolled his eyes and let out an exasperated sigh. "You've just implicated yourself in Eric's murder. Whether you did it or not, there are now *two* witnesses who heard you say it, Margie. I'll deal with it myself," he said.

All of his men and Marjorie took a step back.

"Give me a gun." Larry took the gun offered him from one of his men. "Get a drop cloth. These two will disappear, everyone will think they were the ones who did it and they skipped town, case closed."

At that moment things felt surreal. It was if everything began moving in slow motion. Once again I felt that sensation of my life flashing before my eyes. It hadn't been a good year for me.

But before I could continue with my internal lament we heard a door close, then voices, and from around the corner appeared none other than Reg Mathers who seemed to show up wherever we were. I was beginning to wonder if he was tracking us.

"Fuckin' seriously?" Larry groaned. "Reg, what the fuck are you doin' here?"

"I'm here for these two," Reg said without skipping a beat. "Let's go into the back room and talk about it."

Marjorie, Larry, and Reg disappeared into the back of the warehouse and all we could hear were muffled voices. At one point it sounded like they were arguing, but I can't be sure because one of Larry's henchmen showed up with a tarp and spread it out on the ground behind Mike and I. As it crinkled behind us my hair stood on end. I refused to look back, even though it was tempting to see where my body would lie. My heart was pounding so hard it hurt. I wasn't ready to die.

When they returned, Larry didn't seem so hell-bent on killing us and Marjorie seemed her normal, clueless, carefree, egotistical self.

Reg gave them a look then turned to us, "You two come with me."

"My gun," Mike said to the man who had taken his gun.

The guy looked at Larry, then at Reg, then at Mike. Reg reached out his hand. The guy handed it to Reg without question. It was creepy how they all seemed to be communicating symbiotically. Of course it was also clear that Reg got around and he was both respected and feared. Or it appeared that was the case because people got out of his way and he seemed to be able to bend them to his will. It was probably his dominant nature, I mused. Some males were just alphas no matter the situation.

Reg took Mike's gun and started walking, prompting Mike and I to follow.

"Here, give me my gun," Mike said to Reg when we were finally outside.

"In a minute, get in the car. We have to get the hell out of here now before he changes his mind." Reg led us to a black four door sedan in the parking area. There was someone in the driver's seat. "Get in the back."

"Our car is right around the corner," Mike started.

Reg whirled around with a concerned look on his face. "Mike, look, I know these people. I just saved your ass in there. Just get in the car, we'll drive away and in a few hours, once this place has cleared, we can come back and get the car. All of our lives depend on it."

Mike backed down, opened the back door and let me slide in first. He got in right behind me. The second he pulled the door closed and Reg was sitting in the passenger seat, the car started moving. That's when I realized the woman driving was Alyssa's friend Megan, from *Leather and Lace.*

Reg must have noticed me looking at Megan because he said, "You remember Megan? My girlfriend."

"Oh. Yeah." I remembered her alright. I just hadn't known she was Reg's girlfriend.

Mike merely grunted in acknowledgement.

"Oh," Reg reached into his coat pocket and pulled out Mike's gun, handing it to him. "Sorry I had to take that. I heard from some of the folks on Damien's side of the fence that you two had found Margie and I knew you'd come out here and what would happen."

Mike immediately put his gun back in the shoulder holster under his jacket. "You knew where she was all along?"

"Not initially, but I found out. I know the kind of people they are. I don't go looking for them and I should have told you two to keep your noses clean and not to look for them either." He nodded to Megan. "I didn't want Megan coming at first because that drags her into their world, too. But I needed a get-away driver and she was the only one available."

"Let me just call Gary and let him know we're not there." Mike pulled out his cell phone and made the call. After a few seconds he hung up. "I think he turned his damn phone off."

"So how, exactly, did you get them to let us go and not kill us?" I had to know.

Reg laughed. "They're dangerous, but stupid. I told them you two were wanted by a higher council and I was told to bring you both in."

"Good thing. Thanks," Mike said. "That was close."

"Only if you call having a drop cloth laid out behind you close," I said with a shudder.

Reg shook his head. "He would have done it, too. That Lawrence Becker is a crazy mother fucker. Of course Marjorie isn't too far behind him." He clapped his hands together. "First things first – how about some coffee and a late dinner? There's a place I know up past Red Rocks."

I felt my face pale as he said it. I'd almost died up there, in the park adjacent the amphitheater three months ago. I didn't want to think about it. I forced a polite smile. "I could go for coffee and a bite to eat."

Mike nodded. "That's fine. Then we can get the car and head home. I'll have Marjorie and Lawrence arrested tomorrow. What was Lawrence's last name again?"

"Becker," Reg said. He looked at Megan, "You okay to drive to dinner?"

Megan smiled. "I know where it is, you don't."

"Because I never drive," he told her in a smug tone.

What kind of man didn't drive? *One who compels everyone to do his bidding,* my mind retorted. Whatever, I was just happy we were still alive and far away from Marjorie, Lawrence, and their cronies. I leaned against Mike's shoulder, yawned, and closed my eyes. That was my first mistake.

CHAPTER SIXTEEN
LATE NIGHT SUNDAY, JULY 9

My second mistake was trying to twist out of the elaborate rope bondage I found myself in. I couldn't see anything because I was blindfolded. I'd simply fallen asleep. Long enough to find myself bound and blindfolded, but not gagged.

My initial, sexually repressed and paranoid thought was that Mike and Reg were playing a game at my expense. "Come on you guys. This isn't funny. Untie me."

I was on the ground, lying in the dirt. I could smell the dry earth beneath me and feel the cool night breeze across my face. We were in the mountains somewhere.

Footsteps came toward me. "I really hate having to do this to you two. You're really a nice couple and perhaps, had things turned out differently, we could have all been friends. But I had to get rid of Baca. That son-of-a-bitch knew too much about my business and he was charging me two thousand a month to keep him from going to the police. Enter you two, problem solved. But sadly now I need to make you two disappear."

"Reg," I heard Megan whisper.

"Go sit in the car, Megan," he said firmly.

"Don't do it, Megan. Don't let him kill us," I told her. I heard her light footfalls move quickly toward the car and I heard the door open and close.

"Relax," Reg said.

"Fuck you Reg! You're going to kill me and you want me to relax? Why didn't you just let Marjorie and Larry kill us?" I was really incensed by the audacity he had, but it didn't surprise me. Reg was a typical arrogant alpha male who expected everyone to bask in the glory of his give-a-fuck.

"See, it's very important that you and your boyfriend really do disappear, and I don't trust idiots to do what needs to be done right. I'd just as soon do it myself to make sure it's dealt with," he said.

"Margie and Larry will turn on you in a heartbeat," I shot back.

"They won't do any such thing. They think there is a higher power involved here. Dumb people are easy to manipulate like that. I solved their problem in not having to worry about you two turning them in for attempted murder, you two disappear and people think you committed the murder and skipped town, and everyone else lives happily ever after."

"Wow, you really are an arrogant psychopath." I almost regretted it the second I said it. Reg was unpredictable, after all.

"You create your own reality here Elizabeth. You can fight this, and die in a state of distress, or accept your fate, submit to it, and die peacefully," he said with a flourish. He almost sounded like a cheesy narrator on one of those meditation CD's you can get in the bargain bin at the metaphysical store. "I have been trying to teach you about submission since we first met, but I see none of it has sunk in. Submission takes a great deal of strength and courage. But you have a great deal of self-doubt and fear."

"Gods damn-it. Untie me right now! You'll get submission from my cold, dead body." It was a lame thing to say, I know, but what else could I do? Beg for my life? Well, I could have, but I didn't. That's not my style. Instead I found myself worried about Mike. "Where's Mike?"

"Don't worry about that," Reg started. "I'm going to make it quick and painless. I'll knock you out like I did your cop boyfriend and I'll shoot you while you're unconscious. I'm not a rank criminal void of emotion or compassion. We can do this humanely."

Did that mean he'd already killed Mike? That didn't make me feel any better. I felt an immediate sense of fear and panic. Despite my attempts to face death straight on I knew I was going to be sobbing in a matter of seconds.

The beginning was the end. Of all the stupid things I could have thought at the end of my life, this was it. I felt the clay Lucifuge amulet I wore press hard against my left breast, reminding me that it was because of those damn amulets I was in this mess to begin with. Beneath me the unyielding rocky ground dug into my flesh. Above me, the psychopath who'd murdered Mike loaded the gun.

That was the last thing I remembered.

It was the lights, the noise, the throbbing pain in the side of my head or a combination of all three that brought me out of unconsciousness. I tried to open my eyes but the blast of light shot pain through my skull.

"This one's awake now," a man said.

Then I heard a familiar voice. "Liz, can you hear me?" It was Gary Smith.

I was so relieved to hear Gary's voice. "Where's Mike?"

"Next ambulance over having some water."

"He's not shot?"

"No. He just has a nasty bump that matches yours."

"Did you get Reg?"

"We did. One Reginald Mathers. He's cuffed and on his way out."

I tried to sit up, only to find myself dizzy and nauseated. I couldn't move my head and I could feel the neck brace restricting my movement.

"Stay down. We have to take you to the hospital to have your head x-rayed. Make sure your skull's not fractured," the paramedic told me.

"Great, I need my head examined."

Gary laughed.

Mike's voice came from my left. He sounded like he just woke up. "So what will you tell your mom about this hospital visit?"

"I'm not telling her anything, she doesn't even know my house was taken out by a tornado," I said. "I don't need additional stress. How's your head?"

"It fuckin' hurts. I reached for my gun to stop him, actually pulled the trigger, but my clip was empty. He must have unloaded my clip when he had my gun. I can't believe I didn't check it when I took it back from him."

I could hear Mike patting around for his gun.

"I've got your gun, Mike. I see you didn't give me this one," Gary told him.

"That's my personal gun, it's not standard issue. It's registered. You said Baca was killed with a police issued revolver. I gave you the two I had."

Gary didn't touch that. "Yeah, well, you both need to go to the hospital and make sure neither of you have cracked skulls. Your friend Megan was very helpful and was wearing a wire the entire time. We caught everything Reg said and did on tape, even a confession. Good thing he's a megalomaniac. He bragged about it. Not surprisingly we also think we have the murder weapon in the Baca case so you'll get your other guns back Monday. It looks like he was going to try to make you guys' deaths look like a murder-suicide. We got here just after he knocked Liz out. A minute more and one of you might be dead right now."

I opened my eyes and sat up this time. I really wanted to get the stupid neck brace off. My head throbbed painfully and I was thirsty as hell. "I have a question – what did Reg really tell Marjorie and Larry?"

"Easy – according to Megan he told them he would happily solve their problem for them so no one ever knew they killed Eric Baca." Gary shrugged.

"But Reg killed Baca," I protested.

"Yeah, but he told them he could easily pin it on them if he wanted to," Gary clarified.

"I have never run across so many people blackmailing so many people," Mike said with a groan. He was in a neck brace, too, I noticed. "I'd like to pistol whip that son-of-a-bitch."

"I think we all agree with you, man. If it's any consolation he did trip and fall and hit the side of the squad car with his head on his way in." Gary gave Mike a sympathetic shrug. "On the up side it turns out Reginald was working with the Russian mafia stealing cars and parts. That was a huge break for the organized crime division. That also seems to be the dirt that Eric Baca had on him and was blackmailing him with. So it appears we've solved several cases here."

"Aren't you proud of yourself? And when were you going to tell me all this?" Mike still held his head, but he seemed to be feeling better than I was. He had a smile on his face. "Like when did you plan on telling me Megan was wearing a wire for you guys?"

"She came into the station with that Alyssa you two are always hanging out with. We dealt with it. I thought it would be best if you didn't know so there was plausible deniability. No one can say you planted anything or led him into a confession or anything like that. Trust me, man, you're in the clear after this. As a matter-of-fact your captain wants you in his office as soon as you're cleared by a doctor and you've had a good night's sleep. So Monday morning would be my guess."

"What about Margie and Larry," I asked.

"Yeah, if you can find my phone, I recorded the entire conversation we had with them. I want them charged with conspiracy to commit murder." Mike took the bottle of water one of the police officers handed him.

"We should really get these two to the ER to be looked at," the paramedic told Gary, then protested, "They shouldn't have any water, that's the rules."

"But I'm really thirsty and I'll even sign a waiver saying you didn't give me water," I told him, taking the bottled water the officer handed me. The officer just rolled his eyes at the paramedic's protests and moved back toward his patrol car.

Before the paramedic could further protest I had the bottle uncapped and was drinking from it. It's surprising how good water tastes when you're thirsty. Despite the throbbing on the side of my head when I tried to tip my head back with a neck brace, no easy task I assure you, I somehow managed to drink half the bottle.

Gary nodded and said, "I'll meet you guys at the hospital and take you home when you're done there." He raised an eyebrow at the paramedic. "Really, man, don't worry about it. I'll tell the doctors I gave them the water if it becomes an issue."

"I just don't want to lose my job," the paramedic muttered, trying to usher Mike and I into the ambulance.

"We might need a ride tomorrow to pick up the car," Mike called after Gary. Mike was terribly worried about the car. Probably because it was currently the only car we had between the two of us.

"We'll figure it out. First you two are going to the hospital and if there's no hospital stay, you're both getting some rest before we worry about anything else," Gary said matter-of-fact. We weren't getting away with anything as long as he was around.

A half hour later we found ourselves in the emergency room on watch. They ran a bunch of tests and kept us awake, and by seven-thirty Sunday morning we were exhausted and released from the hospital none worse for the wear. Luckily neither of us had severe concussions. Evidently Reg didn't know how to properly pistol whip a person. At best, he had only temporarily knocked each of us out, leaving a nasty bump in the process.

CHAPTER SEVENTEEN
SUNDAY NIGHT, JULY 9

I don't remember much after my head touched the pillow. When I finally woke up it was dark outside and the blue glow of the clock on the nightstand was the only light in the room. Feeling strangely alone, I reached out to touch Mike. He wasn't there. I heard voices in the living room. I sat upright, listened a few minutes, then got up and wiped the sleep from my eyes. After running a brush through my hair and making sure I looked halfway decent I emerged from the bedroom and cautiously made my way down the hallway to the living room.

I saw Alyssa first and relaxed. It was just Alyssa and Gabe. Megan was with them. Mike and Gary sat on the other end of the room. Between all of them sat the altar, the mantel clock and the painting I'd gotten from Marjorie.

"So she was using these as portals to watch you and Mike? That's so creepy. I can't believe they're bonded, too," Alyssa said.

I stood at the edge of the room looking at them. "So how are we going to do it?"

Gabe spoke up. "We're going to burn all of this. We already took the amulets, encased them in resin, and threw them down the mine shaft up on my uncle's property. Hopefully that eliminates anyone getting ahold of cursed or bonded objects. This stuff is just bonded. Burning it should do it. My friend Dave said we could use the incinerator at his work to get rid of this stuff. We'll take it tonight and I'll drop it off to him in the morning."

"How you doing, babe?" Mike looked at me with concern.

I must have looked worse than I thought because everyone was staring at me. "A little headache, that's all." I turned to Megan then. "Thank for what you did, Megan."

I didn't want her to think her contribution to me and Mike being alive had gone unnoticed.

"I would have never allowed him to hurt you guys. If I had known he killed a guy I would have turned him in immediately," Megan said. She looked as though she was still experiencing a bit of disbelief. She had been dating a murderer, after all.

"At least you found out before things got serious," I said, trying to find Alyssa's optimism.

Alyssa began laughing and Megan shook her head, her own smile spreading over her face ever so slowly.

My stomach growled. Evidently I was hungrier than I realized.

With that, Gabe jumped up. "Okay, ladies, let's get this stuff into my Jeep."

"You need a hand?" Mike asked as Gary got up to offer assistance.

"Nah, we got it," Gabe assured him.

Alyssa grabbed me and hugged me. "I'm so glad you didn't die, again."

I couldn't help but laugh. "Me too."

She scooped up the painting and the mantel clock and the three of them left leaving Gary, Mike and I standing in the living room.

"I'm starving," I announced.

"Gary brought burgers and fries. They're in the kitchen," Mike said. "I'm so glad that shit is out of this house. We're never taking anymore used *crap* from people again, Liz," he told me.

I nodded, even though he couldn't see me. I was already elbow deep in the bag of burgers Gary brought. Snagging two cheeseburgers and a fries from the bag, and soda from the fridge, I sat down at the kitchen table and ate the first meal I'd had in over twenty-four hours. On the second burger I was starting to feel a bit full. I looked up at the clock on the microwave. It was already nine-thirty.

Gary popped his head into the kitchen. "See you tomorrow Liz!"

"Bye, Gary! Thanks for the burgers and for saving us," I said with a grin.

"Anytime, sweetie." He said his farewell's to Mike and then he left. Finally the two of us were alone.

I finished eating and went into the living room, sitting down on the couch next to Mike.

He put his arm around me and we sat in contented silence. Finally, he was the one who spoke first. "We really need a vacation away from our chaotic life. Maybe a week getaway somewhere."

I took a deep breath and thought about the money I had sitting in the savings account, then the fact that I no longer had a house. Then the point that I was using up a good cache of my vacation time and I still hadn't told my parents about my house. I threw caution to the wind. "Maybe someplace neither of us has been before?"

He nodded.

As if in response my cell phone rang. It was in my purse under the coffee table. I reached down and picked it up. Never mind it was another unknown number, this time with a California area code. "Liz Tanner, amateur detective and purveyor of getting herself into impossible situations."

Mike snickered and smacked my leg playfully.

The dignified and somewhat uptight female voice on the other end of the line said, "Ms. Tanner, my name is Kylie Ramone. Perhaps you've heard of me?"

I think my heart stopped for a second. Heard of her? I *loved* Kylie Ramone. She was, in my opinion, the queen of action movies. But what was she doing calling me at nine-thirty at night? In all fairness it was eight-thirty in California. "Yes, of course. What can I do for you?" A huge grin spread over my lips. I couldn't help it.

"I have an interesting dilemma that I need your help with. I was given your name by Gary Martin. He's our regional OTS advisor here in California." She whispered the last part as if it was something she didn't want someone else in the room to overhear.

My mind raced. I actually didn't know anyone in any of the California sects very well. "Oh, Gary, right," I lied.

"Here's the deal, I have a haunted house. I'd like it investigated and cleared if possible, and..." she paused as if she was holding back. "I would prefer someone of *my own faith* perform the investigation and clearing. That's why I called you. The rumor is you're good with necromancy and you can be trusted to keep my religious preference to yourself..."

I gulped, realizing I couldn't stop smiling. "Oh, um, of course. My team and I would have no problems signing non-disclosure agreements."

"Oh good!" She sounded relieved. "How many are on your team?"

"Four," I said matter-of-fact, realizing I was agreeing to something that none of my friends nor Mike had agreed to yet. I was also acting like this was something I did all the time. It wasn't. I was, in my own opinion, a neophyte necromancer at best. It was Alyssa who was the wicked talented necromancer. I was merely what some people in our circle of Daemonolater friends called 'an authority' on all things occult.

"Would August second work for you?"

"That works," I said, hoping that would be plenty of time for the four of us to arrange vacation time, and it would give me enough time to work out my house issues and Mike enough time to make sure he was cleared of any and all charges in the Baca case. Things were looking up.

"I'll arrange for four plane tickets to be sent to you then. You can stay here at the house and you can have full use of the pool and grounds while you're here. Even do some sight-seeing if you like since the activity is mostly at night. It's Beverly Hills, lots to do here and Hollywood is a quick hop-skip-and-a-jump away," she assured me as if her being Kylie Ramone wasn't enough to draw me there.

"Okay. Thank you," I told her. I took the phone into the spare bedroom that I was using as a temporary office to look up Gary Martin on my computer. I just wanted to make sure it was legitimate and to finish giving her the details. As I hung up the phone I turned back toward the living room to find Mike leaning in the doorway.

"What was that?" he asked. He didn't look particularly happy.

"Remember that getaway we were just talking about?"

He nodded and lifted an eyebrow.

"How do you feel about a week in Beverly Hills staying at Kylie Ramone's house?" I was still grinning ear to ear. My face was starting to hurt.

"Seriously? *The* Kylie Ramone?" He gave me a wary look. "What's the catch?"

I shrugged. "We have to sign non-disclosure agreements and we have to do a haunting investigation and clear her house of spirits, ghosts, or whatnot. Fun and low key, right?"

He raised his eyebrow again. "Ghosts?"

I laughed. Always the skeptic. "Yes, ghosts."

"Are you going to verify all this?"

"I'm on it," I told him. I had Gary Martin's number already tapped into my phone. I tapped send. It rang only once before a man picked up. "Hi, Mr. Martin? This is Liz Tanner from OTS..." I started.

I saw Mike shake his head and vaguely heard him say, before walking back toward the living room, "Beverly Hills, huh? Good, I need a vacation but I was hoping it would be without the ghosts, or daemons, or...."

His voice trailed off as he retreated down the hallway.

Ω

Preview
Rising Darkness

An OTS Mystery

CHAPTER ONE
THURSDAY, AUGUST 2

To say Kylie Ramone's allegedly haunted Beverly Hills estate was large would have been an understatement. This was no mere house; it was a mansion. Of course I wasn't told this over the phone. Ms. Ramone had specifically said *house*. I suppose I should have expected a mansion though. She was only the most famous female action film star of the decade. An awed silence fell over the four of us as the SUV pulled into the long driveway leading up to the *house*. Suddenly I felt extremely lower middle class in the jeans, tennis shoes, and blue v-neck blouse I wore.

Mike let out a low whistle. "Damn. It's huge."

"That's what she said," Gabe joked, half distracted by the monstrous mansion that loomed ahead of us.

Alyssa let out a nervous giggle. She turned to me suddenly. "I bet the pool is ginormous!"

"Don't forget what we're here to do," I paused lowering my voice and choosing my words carefully in front of the driver, "This is a *working* vacation you guys," I reminded them. An all-expenses-paid working vacation, but still work even if it was of the paranormal variety.

Alyssa, who wore a pair of black slacks and a smart button down blouse with shoes that carried the name of some designer, rubbed her hands together. "I am totally ready to do this job. Have I mentioned how much I love you for including us in this?"

She gave me a quick side hug as we pulled up to the door. A young, dark-haired woman wearing a suit and carrying a tablet computer started down the stairs toward us. The driver got out and began unloading our luggage and Gabe opened the door so we could file out.

The woman looked at me, then at Alyssa. "Which of you is Elizabeth?"

Alyssa pointed out me and I stepped forward. "That's me."

She took my hand and gave it a firm shake. "I'm Jenna Weiss, Ms. Ramone's personal assistant. She's at a photo shoot this afternoon, so she put me in charge of getting you all settled. I hope your trip went well?"

I nodded, trying to remain as professional as possible. "It did, thank you. We really appreciate the driver coming to get us from the airport."

"James," she nodded toward the driver, "Will be at your disposal for the duration of your stay. Anywhere you want to go, he'll take you. Ms. Ramone said it was the least she could offer in exchange for the work you'll be doing."

"Thanks," I beamed. It was a good thing because Mike had initially planned to rent a car. But after seeing LA traffic and knowing how aggressively Mike drove, I was thankful Ms. Ramone insisted on providing us with all transportation.

Gabe picked up his carefully packed cases of ghost hunting equipment from the curb. It was because of those cases that we spent two hours going through airport security in Denver. Gabe made us each carry one onto the plane because he was convinced that if we put them through baggage check we'd end up a few pieces of equipment short by the time we reached Los Angeles. He was probably right. The infrared cameras, thermometers, digital cameras, digital voice recorders, EMF detectors, motion alarms, computer, and walkie talkies probably amounted to a small fortune. Nonetheless we made it, equipment intact, and Gabe, who ghost-hunted as a hobby, was happy as a clam.

Mike helped Gabe with the remaining cases of equipment. Alyssa and I grabbed our suitcases and together the four of us followed Ms. Weiss into the grand marbled entrance of house. The foyer was breathtaking and looked like something out of a movie.

Alyssa let out a low whistle. "I take it this isn't the cheap look-alike marble," she said.

Ms. Weiss laughed. "No, it's real Carrara from Tuscany. Let's go upstairs and I'll show you to your rooms"

We were halfway up the foyer staircase when I felt the hair on my arms stand on end and a cold chill run through me. I turned to look down below just in time to see a hovering black mass disappear into a closed door. I stared at the door, unsure at first what it was I'd just seen.

"Liz..." Alyssa's voice called down to me. I looked up to see that everyone else was already on the second floor and only Alyssa had stopped to wait for me. "What's wrong?"

"I just thought I saw something." I shook my head and hurried up the stairs to catch up.

Following Alyssa, we soon rejoined the men and Ms. Weiss going down a long hallway that led to the second floor of the west wing of the house.

When the hall came to a stop, Ms. Weiss pushed open a door and motioned toward us. "Forgive me for prying but are you couples or, um, single?"

"Oh," Alyssa jumped in. "Gabe and I will share a room and Liz and Mike will share one, too."

I nodded, looking into the large bedroom beyond the doorway.

"Well two of you in here, then. It has its own bathroom suite, and," she stepped across the hallway and opened another door revealing another large bedroom, "two of you in here. Same thing, it has its own bathroom. I'll leave you to get settled and then if you'd like to meet in the sitting room downstairs in an hour I can give you the tour."

I nodded, still overwhelmed. "Sitting room?"

"Oh, of course." Ms. Weiss shook her head, seemingly embarrassed. "It's the first room on the left just off the foyer as you come in the main doors."

"Thank you," I said.

Mike gave Ms. Weiss a polite nod of acknowledgement, Alyssa gave her a mumbled word of thanks and Gabe bolted into the first bedroom. "This is me and Alyssa's room!"

Mike nodded and turned toward the second room. He motioned me toward the door. "After you, gorgeous."

I didn't really care for the second room one bit. There was something about it. Slowly ambling into the room I stood next to the bed and looked around. It had been decorated in what I guessed to be old Victorian by the scrollwork. One dresser had a full mirror attached to it. Another bureau sat directly in front of the bed and on top of it stood a flat panel television. The windows were dressed with a thick covering of maroon satin and white lace. The ceiling was high and I immediately noticed the crown molding. It wasn't an ugly room by any means. It just felt *off*. Then I mused how I always wanted a house with crown molding.

My own house was currently in the midst of being rebuilt after a tornado had destroyed it only a month earlier. Mike and I had talked about the possibility of him selling his place, me selling mine, and us buying a house together. Of course *that* level of commitment made me a bit queasy just thinking about it. I'd never been this serious about a man, ever. But after the stress of our last adventure, living together had become routine and we were in sync. I think we were both enjoying co-habitation and I didn't feel in a rush to get back into my own place. Mike didn't seem in a hurry for me to go, either.

Mike set all the suitcases next to the dresser and turned to look at me. "This room is very, um, frilly."

I laughed. "It's Victorian."

"That's the era it should have stayed in," he said, looking around with a scowl.

"The crown molding is cool," I said, nodding at the ceiling.

He nodded back. "Maybe when we start looking at houses we'll put that on the wish-list."

I smiled. Every time he brought it up he sounded so sure of the idea. I found myself agreeing. Sitting down on the bed I looked at the floor. The floors were wood, but on top of the wood were beautiful area rugs in deep maroon and gold, one on each side of the bed and another in front of the dresser. "And I really want wood floors," I added.

He didn't say anything, just looked at the floors and nodded.

I got up and started toward the bathroom. Mike followed. Turning on the light I was kind of surprised to see the crisp white pedestal sink, toilet and shower stall. The only thing that matched the décor of the bedroom was a freestanding cabinet that contained extra toilet paper, fresh towels and washcloths; the linens were red and gold.

"Well, thank goodness we don't have to use bedpans, water pitchers and basins," Mike said, matter-of-fact.

I laughed. It was just like him to be a smart ass. "Indeed. We should open the drapes. It's dark in here," I said, feeling a bit claustrophobic in the room. I really was hoping opening the drapes would let the light in and make that sense of foreboding go away. Going over to the window, I found the drape pull and opened the drapes, allowing cascades of sunlight to fall over the maroon and gold bedspread.

"You mind if I wash up really quick before we head downstairs for the tour?" Mike gave me a hopeful look.

"Go ahead. I might lie down for a few minutes," I said. "I'm kind of tired from the flight."

"A little jet lag," he nodded and gave me a sympathetic look. "I'll be out in a few and then you can freshen up."

I nodded and turned back toward the window, looking out over the precisely manicured lawn below and beyond that, the pool. Smiling, I mused how Alyssa probably had plans for that pool. She was probably trying on swimsuits now. Making my way back to the bed, I sat on it, surprised at how firm the mattress was. I suppose I'd expected something softer to fit the soft features of the room. Despite this I settled in, enjoying the fullness of the pillow beneath my head. I closed my eyes.

That's when I heard it.

"Elizabeth," it whispered.

My eyes flew open and I sat straight up. I could hear the water running in the bathroom. Mike had the door closed. Scanning the room, I took a deep breath. There was no one there. I shook my head and silently scolded myself for being so jumpy. Sure, the house was big and somewhat creepy, but I was probably feeling residual energy off of the old furniture or something. Or maybe, just maybe, I was allowing the idea of being in a haunted house mess with my brain.

I took another deep breath and settled back into the bed, unable to shake that feeling that I wasn't alone. Something was watching me. That's when I heard the snap and the room went dark as the drapes closed on their own. I jumped up again and this time, two loud bangs sounded on the wall behind me. I let out a startled yelp.

Mike opened the bathroom door. "Babe? You okay?"

"Did you hear that?"

"No. And why'd you close the drape, it's actually pretty dark in here." Mike started toward the window and went about re-opening the drapes.

Meanwhile, I watched the black shadow motion me toward it as it stepped through the door leading into the hallway. My blood ran cold. "Mike," I whispered, "There's something really awful in this house and it knows why we're here."

About the Author

Audrey Brice is the pseudonym of a renowned Daemonolatress and practicing magician who has been performing her artes since the mid-eighties. She lives with her husband and several cats along the front range of the beautiful Rocky Mountains.

Also by **Audrey Brice**

Outer Darkness

When socialite Chloe Brigid is murdered and the crime seems to have occult overtones, outed daemon worshiper Senator Steve Mitchell is arrested. It's up to magician Elizabeth Tanner, the public figurehead of the Ordo Templi Serpentis, to find out who outed the senator and who killed Chloe Brigid before the senator is falsely accused of the crime and The Order is investigated. What she finds, however, is not what she expects. The killer's attention soon turns toward her. Will she be able to help the police find the killer before she becomes the next victim?

Forthcoming:

Rising Darkness
Thirteen Covens

By Audrey Brice as **Anne O'Connell**

Training Amy

When Amy starts her new job at a book shop she has no idea what kind of merchandise her two bosses have stored in a private back room for select customers. She's never been allowed back there. One night, when she's closing shop alone she decides to take a look. Big mistake. Brad and Eric (her bosses) catch her snooping around. They don't tolerate rule-breakers and Amy must be punished. Will her secret desires plunge her deeper into their world? Or will she run back to the safety of her normal life and the dull boyfriend who has a dark side of his own?

Publisher's Note: This book contains explicit sexual content, graphic language, and situations that some readers may find objectionable: BDSM theme and content includes: dubious consent, bondage, spanking, toys, anal play, and menage m/f/m and m/f/f.

Other Titles:
Weekend Captive
Sincerely, Megan
Nice Girls Don't
My Neighbor Enslaved

Forthcoming:
Switched
DOM359
Her Demon Lover

By Audrey Brice as **S. J. Reisner**

Left Horse Black

For centuries, the zealot Kersian sorcerers have abducted innocent women and children for sacrifice to their 'no name' god, and have waged war upon Danaria's sorcerers. Now, they are covertly usurping the thrones of human-ruled kingdoms to do the unthinkable; they are building a massive human army to assist them in destroying Danaria's sorcerer bloodlines in an attempt to save their own. Armed with nothing more than meager weapons, untrained sorcery, and mere instinct, a troubled human prince, an inept Danarian sorceress, and their friends, rise up and become the world's last hope to stop the Kersians, and save the sorcerers' dying race. Will they succeed?

Other Titles:

Warrior's Blood Red

Forthcoming:

Eagle's Talon Gray
Seeress of Prylyn

By Audrey Brice as **S. Connolly**

Curses, Hexes & Crossing

Renowned Daemonolatress S. Connolly explores the taboo topic of Execration Magick from a unique "darker path" perspective. This book covers cursing from Ancient Egypt to modern times and gives the modern magician plenty to consider when it comes to cursing, hexing, and crossing enemies; as well as learning to break bad habits and curse bad situations. Also included is a section about protections, how to break curses, how to clear one's personal space of negativity, and simple methods for psychic self-defense.

Other Titles:
The Complete Book of Demonolatry
The Daemonolater's Guide to Daemonic Magick
The Art of Creative Magick
Honoring Death
Infernal Colopatiron
Daemonolatry Goetia

Forthcoming:
Keys of Ocat
Grimoirium Daemonolatrie

www.ingramcontent.com/pod-product-compliance
Lightning Source LLC
Chambersburg PA
CBHW071251250626
47163CB00002B/420